THE LAST RIDE

LES SAVAGE, JR.

SAGEBRUSH
Large Print Westerns

First published in the United States by Five Star

First Isis Edition
published 2018
by arrangement with
Golden West Literary Agency

*A catalogue record for this book is available
from the British Library.*

ISBN 978–1–78541–394–0 (pb)

Published by
F. A. Thorpe (Publishing)
Anstey, Leicestershire

Set by Words & Graphics Ltd.
Anstey, Leicestershire
Printed and bound in Great Britain by
T. J. International Ltd., Padstow, Cornwall

This book is printed on acid-free paper

THE LAST RIDE

Pothooks Marrs is the day cook at the Dallas café
Co'   Ne   xpert
rop   80   from
the   irder,
he'   1. But
wh   eet, it
see   1. For
Co 19/11/22   San
An   one
of 1   Could
it b   ffered
a jo   e Bar
spr   . And
the: none
oth

SPECIAL MESSAGE TO READERS

THE ULVERSCROFT FOUNDATION
(registered UK charity number 264873)
was established in 1972 to provide funds for
research, diagnosis and treatment of eye diseases.
Examples of major projects funded by
the Ulverscroft Foundation are:-

- The Children's Eye Unit at Moorfields Eye Hospital, London
- The Ulverscroft Children's Eye Unit at Great Ormond Street Hospital for Sick Children
- Funding research into eye diseases and treatment at the Department of Ophthalmology, University of Leicester
- The Ulverscroft Vision Research Group, Institute of Child Health
- Twin operating theatres at the Western Ophthalmic Hospital, London
- The Chair of Ophthalmology at the Royal Australian College of Ophthalmologists

You can help further the work of the Foundation
by making a donation or leaving a legacy.
Every contribution is gratefully received. If you
would like to help support the Foundation or
require further information, please contact:

THE ULVERSCROFT FOUNDATION
The Green, Bradgate Road, Anstey
Leicester LE7 7FU, England
Tel: (0116) 236 4325

website: www.foundation.ulverscroft.com

CHAPTER
ONE

Marrs saw Sadie push through the heat-fogged doors of the Cowman's Rest and he started fumbling doughnuts onto a plate for her usual order. Then he stopped. He stopped and stared through the window at the man who had appeared on the other side of Jackson Street. A fat man, standing on the curb in front of the Oxbow Saloon. A prodigiously fat man wearing a pair of dirty buckskin breeches and letting his long red underwear suffice for his shirt.

Marrs felt a flutter of nausea start way down in his belly. He didn't want to believe it. But there could be no mistake. It was Kettle Cory.

"Gawd," Sadie said, sliding onto a counter stool, "you'd think it was still winter, with that fog coming up off the Trinity." She leaned forward with a tired sigh and put her elbows on the counter. Its edge dug deeply into the melon-like bulges of her breasts. "When is Dallas going to get warm, Pothooks?"

Marrs didn't answer. He was sicker now, with sickness compounded of fear and rage and helplessness that went back into the years. When Sadie saw the expression on his face, she followed his gaze out through the misty window to where Kettle Cory stood.

"What is it, Pothooks? Your dead uncle?"

He wheeled about suddenly, putting the plate down so carelessly the doughnuts spilled off. He walked swiftly down the counter to his coat. He pulled it off the hook and lifted the counter gate and stepped through and dropped it with a *bang*. At the other end of the counter, Bob Warren looked up from his ledgers.

"What's the matter?" he said.

Marrs was walking swiftly toward the side door. "Call Len. I'm knocking off."

"Knocking off? You just got here."

"I'm knocking off," Marrs said. There was a sound of desperation to his voice. Warren ducked beneath the counter gate at his end, blocking Marrs off and grabbing his arm.

"Wait a minute. You know Len didn't quit till two this morning. I can't get another cook, Pothooks."

Marrs tried to pull free and get by him, but Warren pulled him around with a jerk. "What the hell, if you're sick, I'll call a doctor."

"I said let me go!" Marrs's voice was savage, and he swung an elbow into the boss' belly. It flung Warren back into the counter violently. Marrs took one look over his shoulder at the man across the street, then lunged for the side door. He had reached it, with his hand on the knob, before he realized that he could not go out this way, either. The door opened onto a deadend alley. The only way out was into the street, and Kettle would see him. He stood rigidly there, still facing the door. His breathing made a hoarse sound in the room.

2

Warren had straightened up, leaning against the counter, wheezing softly with the pain of the belly blow. He was a tall string bean of a man with a hollow-cheeked, jaundiced face and red-rimmed eyes.

"Pothooks," he said. "What the hell is it? I never seen you like this before."

Slowly Marrs turned around to face him. He was so broadly framed that he appeared shorter than his actual five feet ten. Long use and countless washings had taken all the blue out of his Levi's and denim shirt. They were chalk-white at the elbows and knees and the shirt was so shrunken from its original size that the thick muscles of his neck and shoulders had split out the seams. He was the black-haired kind whose jaws would hold a bluish sheen no matter how often he shaved, and the hue spread like a shadow down into his corded neck. The heavy lids of his eyes gave them a sullen, withdrawing look, and they moved briefly to Warren as he spoke.

"I'm sorry, Bob," he said in a tight voice. "Off my feed or something."

He edged slowly back toward the gate, trying not to look out the windows again. He went behind the counter, hung his coat up, walked down to the grill, and put the doughnuts back on the plate for Sadie. He felt like a rat in a trap. He couldn't go out either door without Kettle's seeing him. Did the man know he was here? He couldn't conceive any other reason for Kettle's being this far north. *Why keep up the cat-and-mouse, damn you? Why not come on over and finish it up?*

3

Marrs realized how intently Sadie was watching him. He put the doughnuts on the counter for her and turned for the coffee pot. The woman glanced over her shoulder at Warren, who had gone back to his accounting, still frowning in a mystified way at Marrs. Then Sadie leaned forward again, the counter digging that deep crease in the plump flesh of her breasts. Her voice was too low for Warren to hear.

"I could get him out of the way, Pothooks."

"What?"

She straightened up, looking hurt. "Don't take on so high and mighty. I still got my charm. I go over there. Wiggle a hip. He'd follow me, you bet."

He realized what she meant. His chin dipped down. It made white grooves of tension in the bluish sheen of his jaw.

"Never mind," he said. Kettle was too sharp for that. He'd know when he was being lured away.

"I never thought I'd see you scared of anything human," she said.

"Forget it. Here's your coffee."

The door *banged* sharply. Marrs's head jerked up and he spilled the coffee. But it was only a railroader, hands stuffed in the pockets of his Levi jacket.

"Some of those splatter dabs, Pothooks, and a gallon of java."

Marrs wiped up the spilled coffee and turned to pour batter from a cracked china crock onto the griddle. He was facing the window now. He could not help the slow lifting of his eyes. The fat man was turning, pushing through the batwings of the Oxbow, disappearing

4

inside. That didn't help. He could still see across the street.

Sadie leaned over the counter, speaking softly. "That part of the back trail, Pothooks?"

Marrs glanced toward the railroader bantering with Warren at the other end of the long counter. "Let it go, will you?" he said.

"Don't get sore," Sadie said. "It don't make no difference to me. Only a gal can't help wondering. You've been here ten months now and there ain't a soul knows more about you than your name." She looked at his hands. They were hairy and corded, with faint white scars making a pattern all over their backs. "I've seen enough cowpokes, Pothooks. Those are rope scars. A cow camp cook don't do that much roping, either. You must have worked cattle. I've seen the way you look down Jackson whenever a trail herd's camped across the river, too. There's one called the Pickle Bar out there now. You hear the cattle bawling, them cowpokes come in smelling like a stable. I see the look on your face . . ."

"Forget it, I'm asking you, forget it!"

Pothooks spoke so sharply that Warren raised his head from his accounts. "Sadie," he said, "don't ride him, will you? A cook like Pothooks only comes once in a lifetime. I want to keep him."

"I wasn't doing nothing," Sadie said sullenly.

Marrs flipped the cakes onto a plate, poured tallow on top for butter, carried the plate and a pot of long sweetening down to the railroader. When he got back to Sadie, he found her leaning across the counter again,

5

holding out her empty coffee cup. He took the pot off the grate and began to pour.

"You could tell me, Pothooks," she said in a husky voice. "You know I'd never tell. If it was murder, I'd never . . ."

She broke off at the expression on his face. He looked like a whipped man, and his eyes were wide open for the first time.

"Pothooks," she said, "I didn't mean anything. I was just kidding."

He wheeled away from her, setting the pot down with a *clang*. He stared at the wall, and the knotted muscles made ridges across his back, beneath the chalk-white denim of his shirt.

"Hell," Sadie said, "now you've spoiled my appetite."

She put a dime on the counter and went out the door. Only then did he turn back. The whipped expression faded slowly from his face. He found himself looking across the street again, hardly aware of Sadie's blowzy figure stamped against the fogged window, sleazy dress slithering across the wobble of meaty hips as she walked away.

He was filled with the savage impulse to make the break now, to get away from this cat-and-mouse game. But one thing kept him from it. The chance that Kettle Cory was in Dallas for some other reason — the slim possibility that he would have his drink in the Oxbow and then go on. If the man really didn't know Marrs was here, Marrs would be a fool to take the chance of revealing himself. It was a feeble hope, but it was all he had left.

And yet, clinging to it, Marrs couldn't help the questions that pounded at him: *Why, Kettle, after all this time? Are you working for the state now? Or is it Boa? Do they want me dead that bad?*

CHAPTER
TWO

Down Jackson Street, past the station, across the Trinity, out in the lush-grassed bottom lands on the west bank of the river, a thousand Pickle Bar cattle browsed sleepily in the early morning mists. It was cold here, and it stank of rotten bottom mud where the cow camp had been pitched by a lightning-struck hackberry. The chuck wagon and the canvas-topped linchpin stood by the gray ashes of dead cook fires. But there was only one man still lying in his sougan, amid the dozen saddles scattered around the fire for pillows.

Bob Slaughter came awake with someone touching him, and grabbed for his gun. Then, with his hand on the weapon, his sleep-fogged vision was filled with a woman's face — wind-blown taffy hair framed large, gray eyes, and the damp, ripe curve of a rich underlip.

"Gail," he snapped. "Don't you know how to wake a man on the trail yet? I might have thrown down on you."

"All right, Bob," she panted angrily. "Next time I'll stand ten feet back and pelt you with a pebble. The crew's hoorawing the cook down in the river. You've got to stop it. They're mad enough to drown him."

"Not again," groaned Slaughter, pulling himself out of his sougan, fully dressed. He was nearly forty-five, but his long, driving legs in the rumpled striped pants, and his lean pivoting waist held the hard, vital youth of a man fifteen years his junior.

Following Gail through the smoldering cook fires, he ran his hand roughly across the strong, cutting thrust of his jaw, feeling the greasy blond stubble. His long yellow hair fell over a belligerent brow, and the impatient toss of his head, throwing it back, flashed chill little lights across his hard blue eyes. The movement made him wince. A dull ache shot through his temples, and he squinted his eyes, pinching the bridge of his nose. Either the liquor was getting stronger in Dallas, or he was getting older, he didn't know which. He must have slept right through the fuss this morning. He rarely did that, even after a high-heel night.

They skirted the untended trail herd, and Gail pushed through the elderberry. Even in his vague stupor, Bob felt the keen appreciation of her presence. Hair that hung like rich strands of taffy down over her shoulders, and the faded blue cashmere robe failed to hide the mature rondure of her hips, the lissome motion of a body every man on the Chisholm Trail talked of. She had been married to Paul Butler for ten years, and for three years Slaughter had bossed their Pickle Bar trail herds north to the Kansas markets, and each year he thought she became more desirable to him.

They burst from the brush onto the rich, mucky soil of the Trinity bottoms, and could hear the men shouting and milling around in the shallows of the river. In their midst, Slaughter could make out the surging, struggling figure of the cook. *Don* Vargas was the *vaquero* who claimed to be descended from Spanish royalty — a lithe, slim whip of a youth in fancy *taja* leggings and a frogged *charro* jacket — hopping around on the fringe and shouting.

"Dunk him again! He's been cutting pieces off my saddle for those atrocities he calls steaks ever since we left the Nueces."

The peg-legged man holding the cook by his shirt front had been dubbed Pata Pala by *Don* Vargas, which meant "shovel leg" in Spanish. Despite his handicap, he was the best all-around hand in the crew, and the bully of them to boot. He straddled the biscuit-shooter and put his head under water again.

"Let him go!" shouted Slaughter, descending on them in a vicious, long-legged stride.

"Stay out of this, Slaughter!" called Waco Garrett, holding one hand across his belly as if to ease the pain of some old internal injury so many brush hands carried within them. "You can't palm a pothooks like this off on us. My system's so saturated with that hog belly he's cooked for beef that I sweat straight leaf lard and my hide's so slick I can't keep my leggings on."

"Leave go of him, I said!" roared Slaughter. Reaching the crowd, he pulled Windy aside with one sweeping arm to get at Pata Pala. Windy staggered back and sat down in the water, his mop of white hair falling

10

over his eyes. Slaughter hooked one hand in the peg-legged man's belt and heaved backward. Pata Pala let go of the cook and whirled about before he lost balance. He was taller than Slaughter's six foot one, and twice as big around the waist, a great, beefy bully of a man with a matted roan thatch and a stubble beard so filled with grease and dirt its color was indeterminate. He caught Slaughter's arm in one hand. Slaughter slugged him in the belly. Pata Pala grunted, bent toward Slaughter, raking for his face. Slaughter pulled the Navy Colt from his belt and laid it across the man's face. Pata Pala toppled sideways with a heavy groan, and Slaughter jumped on him before he struck the ground.

Solo Sam had grabbed the sputtering cook, jamming a sopping wet hat into his face, and Windy had risen to boot the biscuit-shooter in his behind. They both stared at Slaughter, and released the cook.

"Now," said Slaughter, holding the gun for whipping, "if anybody else wants to hooraw this pothooks, let him come ahead. I'll whip strips off his face and make jerky of it." They spread away from the choking, gasping cook, staring sullenly at Slaughter. "Vamoose, then," he said finally. "Get back to camp and catch up. If this is what you want, we'll ride without breakfast."

Pata Pala rose sullenly, holding the bloody weal cutting its livid swath through one cheek. His little bloodshot eyes held Slaughter's gaze for a moment, then, without speaking, he wheeled sharply and walked as fast as he could up the bottom slope, hitching the hip of that peg leg forward with each step. The others followed, one by one, until only the cook and Slaughter were left in the water.

"Now get back to your chuck wagon," said Slaughter. "And do something about that cooking of yours."

"There won't be any more cooking," sobbed the bowlegged, bald-pated little man. "I'm through, Slaughter."

"The hell you are," said Slaughter. "You know we can't get another range cook in this town. You're staying, belly cheater, or I'll lay this dewey on you, too."

"Go ahead," snarled the man. "You can beat me all day. It still won't make me stay."

With a curse, Slaughter lunged at him, but Gail cried out from farther up the bank, and slopped into the shallows to grab at him. "Slaughter, let him alone. Haven't you gone far enough already?"

"Far enough! What the hell did you want me to do, kiss their boots?"

"Haven't you got any diplomacy in you?" she said hotly. "You can't drive men like a bunch of cattle, Slaughter. Maybe they had a legitimate quarrel here. You didn't even stop to reason with them."

"You don't know men like I do," he said. "I've been bossing crews for ten years, Gail, and commanding troops for five before that. You've got to make them respect you."

"It isn't respect you win by whipping them at every turn," she said. "You've got to do something more than that. They may fear you and jump whenever you yell, Bob, but I wouldn't call that respect."

12

He realized the cook had left. He caught her elbow, moving her out of the water, putting a check on his anger with great difficulty. "Gail, dear, let's not quarrel like this. I don't want to quarrel with you, you know that. Every boss has a way of handling his men. This is just my way, that's all. It's always worked out."

She stared up at him. "What is it that keeps you driving so hard, Bob? You're afraid to let down one minute. You're past forty, yet you drive yourself like a man half your age."

"A man has to keep stepping to stay at the top," he said.

"Is that it?" she said. "Are you that afraid of slipping?"

"Afraid? Why should I be afraid?"

"I think you are," she said.

He felt the old discomfort under the candid, searching probe of her quiet gray eyes. "You're being very mysterious," he said. "I don't want to talk this way with you. Gail" — his voice sobered — "how is Paul?"

She accepted the abrupt transition without issue, her face darkening. "About the same." She shrugged. "That jolting wagon isn't helping him much."

"Why do you stick with that whining little baby, Gail?"

"He's my husband, Bob."

"He hasn't been your husband for five years and you know it," he said. "He's just been a name on the Pickle Bar checkbook. You've run the outfit as long as I've worked for it. He's just been a whining sniveling bundle of rags in one bed or another to sit beside and nurse and . . ."

"Bob!"

"It's time I spoke out," he said, facing the horror in her eyes. "Don't let any false sentiment come between us, Gail. I know you feel the same way I do. I hear him going for you in that wagon. You don't get a word of thanks. It's all whining and swearing and berating, like an old woman. I don't understand what you saw in him in the first place."

Her eyes seemed to focus on something beyond him, and her voice was barely audible. "He was very handsome."

"When are you going to quit, Gail? You don't owe him anything. He doesn't deserve your life. Waco Garrett leads a normal life with that injury of his. He does the work of two men with his belly hurting him so much most of the time he can't even see. Pata Pala makes out fine with only one leg. They don't go to bed every time it starts bothering them. If Paul can't face it like a man, it shouldn't . . ."

"Bob, stop it."

"I won't. You were meant for something more than that, Gail. You need a man."

Her brows raised. "You, Bob?"

He took her elbows, lifting the weight of her body toward him. "You know how I feel, Gail."

"I can see you don't know how I feel, Bob," she said, pulling away from him. It was no violent effort, but it held an unyielding insistence that caused him to release

14

her. "What makes you keep thinking Paul is the only reason I haven't turned your way?"

A herd of one thousand cattle was shifting about nervously on the bed ground, cropping at weedy grass in a vain effort to fill their bellies. Bob Slaughter moved back through them moodily, a few minutes after Gail had left him there in the bottoms and returned to camp herself. The whole camp was ominously silent until Guy Bedar showed up, coming from behind the chuck wagon on his hairy little bay horse. Narrow enough to take a bath in a shotgun barrel, he had a face as sharp as a Karankawa war hatchet, and kept his lips clamped shut so tightly they made a jump trap look slack. The tattered brim of his horse-thief hat was pinned back against a crown so filthy it looked black, his leather ducking jacket was streaked with grease and tobacco juice, his leggings were caked with mud and droppings.

"Where is everybody?" Slaughter asked him.

"Most of the crew went into Dallas for a meal," said Bedar. "Told me they wouldn't come back till you got them a decent cook. Incidentally a man named Rickett would like to see you over by the grub wagon."

The chuck outfit was about twenty yards this side of the linchpin wagon in which Paul Butler had kept his sickbed since taking cold and a fever on the Colorado near Austin. The two men, standing on this side of the chuck wagon, would be unseen from the linchpin. One of them was a short, thick-set man in a black Prince Albert and a black string tie. He had a square, open face and guileless blue eyes and lips with such a facile twist they reminded Slaughter of the fluted edge around the crust of a pie.

"I'm Harry Rickett," he said. "Perhaps you've heard of me. Or of Thibodaux."

The man he indicated leaned against a wheel in languid indifference, something Creole to the almost womanish beauty of his long-lashed eyes, staring at Slaughter without seeming to see him. The simple black butt of his gun held a quiet, professional competence.

"I've been trying to remember where I'd seen you," Slaughter told Rickett. "You used to run a faro layout in the Alamo."

Rickett's smile faded. "A man has to start somewhere. You should see the Alamo now, Slaughter. Quiet as a churchyard. All of Abilene's dead, for that matter. You know, some claim it was the quarantine regulations and the opposition of the farmers that drew the cattle trade away from Abilene and caused it to decline as a cow town. But those who really know date the beginning of that decline from the year you decided to drive the Pickle Bar to Ellsworth instead of Abilene. Twenty trail bosses followed your lead. I never believed the stories they told about you till then. They said you were the biggest man on the trail. The first up the Chisholm every spring, the spearhead for the whole bunch."

"Do you always grease the axle?" said Slaughter.

"I'm not laying it on *that* thick." Rickett grinned. "It's the truth, and you know it. A man with your reputation, driving for one of the most famous outfits on the trail, constitutes sort of a guiding star. That's why I've come to you, Slaughter. You know what happens to the gambling interests when the cattle stop coming to a town like Abilene. They fold up. They lose money. Not only do they stop making it, their original investments go down the drain. A lot of headaches, Slaughter, a lot of lost fortunes. It happens to every cow town. The trail keeps bending west, and it keeps happening over and over again. Coffeyville, Baxter Springs, Abilene. And now it's happened to Ellsworth. The quarantine line has been moved west of town. Certain far-sighted interests had seen what happened to Abilene and the others, and had prepared to pull out of Ellsworth in time. But this quarantine law fouled up their plans. If no cattle are driven to Ellsworth this spring, the interests I represent will go under with as disastrous results as they did in Abilene."

"And you want me to buck the quarantine?" said Slaughter.

"Isn't he perspicacious, Thibodaux?" asked Rickett.

"Perspicacious," said Thibodaux.

Rickett saw the flush start creeping up Slaughter's neck, and held up a placating hand. "They'll follow you, Slaughter. If you push on to Ellsworth and show this quarantine deadline up for the foolish thing it is anyway, the other trail bosses will be right on your hocks. Five hundred cowboys in the Lone Star district, Slaughter. Listen to the lion roar and buck the tiger. Nothing like a booming trail town for high-heel times."

"Kansas doesn't see anything silly about this quarantine law. They claim Texas cattle are bringing the fever north like a plague."

"Not a case of it in the last six months," Rickett said.

"The quarantine law isn't such a silly thing when there's an army of inspectors and officials backing it up," said Slaughter.

"Not quite an army." Rickett pouted. "Maybe they'd let you slip by anyway, if their palms got a little oily."

"From your money?" asked Slaughter. "What about the grangers? You couldn't pay them off. There's too many."

"You've pushed through worse things than a few sodbusters with rusty old greeners," said Rickett. "What about the time Jared Thorne and his jayhawkers tried to stop you?"

"I lost half the herd and half my crew," said Slaughter. "Which is just what would happen here. It's always the cows that suffer."

"What's a few cows?" said Rickett. "When the other bosses saw you got through, there'd be twenty outfits coming into Ellsworth. With that many on the trail, the farmers wouldn't stand a chance."

"That would be after I got through," said Slaughter. "Losing that many cows would put Pickle Bar on the red side of the ledger for this year. They're skating on thin ice already. I think it would finish Butler if he didn't show profit for this drive."

"It wouldn't finish you," said Rickett. "You'd have enough to establish an outfit of your own, Slaughter. Bigger than the Pickle Bar ever dreamed of being. Get through to Ellsworth and the interests I work for would see to that."

"They won't get a chance to," said Slaughter. "I may have had my high-heel times, Rickett, but when the last boot is empty, no man can say I bunch-quit the outfit I worked for."

"You're getting along, Slaughter," said Rickett. "There won't be many more years of bossing an outfit this size for you. It takes a young man. What then? Back to twenty and found in a 'puncher's saddle. Look what happened to Bert Pierce. Almost as big a man as you on the trail, Slaughter, in his day. They say he's swamping for some saloon in Wichita now. A lot of them go that way, Slaughter, when they get too old for rodding a job this tough."

"I'll be bossing a trail herd when you're getting pitched off a cloud, Rickett . . ." Slaughter halted his guttural explosion, surprised at the vehemence of it. He forced his voice to a strained mutter. "I don't want your proposition. I'm turning west at Red River for Dodge City."

"I've told you the example you provide for the other drivers," said Rickett. "Reach Ellsworth and they'd follow your lead. On the other hand, Dodge City isn't established as a trail town yet. They'll be watching you on that route, too. If you didn't make it to Dodge, a lot of them would turn back to Ellsworth."

"Is that a threat?"

"You interpret it any way you choose," said Rickett. "For my part, I'm just trying to show you how, either way, you'd provide an example. Jared Thorne and his jayhawkers are still active up there, Slaughter. They're a lot stronger than the year they tried to hooraw you.

Last year they tied Pie Cameron to a tree and whipped him to death. When his hands found Pie, they turned back to Texas and left the whole herd for Jared. A lot more grangers over that way, too. Snaky. Mean. Organized. Just as liable to shoot a cowhand as not on sight."

"If you put a bug in their ear," said Slaughter.

"The interests I work for have connections in surprising directions," said Rickett. "They could throw a lot of things your way . . . or *in* your way. Why don't you reconsider? As I say, in either direction, you could provide the example that might well affect the other drivers. But one way you lose, and the other way you win. Only a fool would deliberately put the chips on a losing number."

"And where I win, the Pickle Bar loses," said Slaughter. "I told you where I stood, Rickett. I'm asking you to leave my camp now."

"Don't be a fool, Slaughter . . ."

"Will you get the hell out!" shouted Slaughter. He saw Thibodaux straighten unhurriedly from the chuck wagon, unlacing his fingers from across his belt buckle. Slaughter pulled his elbows back slightly until his hands were pointing inward by his hips, focusing attention on the butt of his gun, thrusting its oak grips from the middle of his belt. "Go ahead," he told Thibodaux. "If that's what's in order now. I'd like you to. I'd like you to very much."

"Not now, Thibodaux," said Rickett. The flannel smile still curled his lips, but for a moment, in his eyes, Slaughter caught the hint of a raw, ruthless force that was totally out of keeping with the oily, genial surface of the man. "But that doesn't necessarily mean never, Slaughter. We'll let you sweat it out through the Indian Nations. That's a wild territory. Lots of things can happen there to change a man's attitude. And here's a thought to take along for the next time we meet. You make your living by what you can do with cattle, and you're one of the best in the game. Thibodaux makes his living by what he can do with a gun, and he's one of the best in the game. I know he would never be foolish enough to try and match you in your field. You'd make him look very silly." He looked at Slaughter's gun butt. Then his eyes raised until they met Slaughter's, and that rippling smile filled his mouth. "I'm sure, after a little thought on the matter, you wouldn't really like him to. Would you now?"

CHAPTER
THREE

East of the Texas and Pacific tracks, the streets of Dallas were filled with mud like slick black wax. Gail Butler turned her little bald-faced bay up Jackson Street, passing a freight outfit stuck hub deep in the ooze, wincing at the blistering profanity of the roaring, laboring teamster and his swamper as they tried to get the mud-caked mules to budge the immense Murphy. She saw Kettle Cory's hairy, heavy-rumped cutting horse hitched among several other animals before the Oxbow Saloon, and turned her mount into the rack. She looked at the mud beneath her feet, reluctant to get off, and bent over the saddle horn, trying to peer over the splintered batwing doors. She couldn't see anything.

At this moment another rider appeared down the street in the same direction from which she had come, showering mud on the cursing teamsters as he cantered by them. It was Bob Slaughter, driving his horse in the same flamboyant, reckless way that he drove himself, pulling it up to a rearing halt before Gail.

"What are you doing in town?" he asked her.

"Trying to get my crew back before they get so drunk we'll be stuck here a week," she said. "And, incidentally, looking for a cook. Kettle's in here. Help me off, will you?"

Reluctantly Slaughter threw his rawhide reins over the dun's hammer head and stepped off, sinking halfway to his knees in the mud. She allowed herself to slide off one side of her animal into his arms. They were strong and hard about her body. She could not deny the excitement his intense masculinity stirred in her. Paul's arms were weak, flaccid.

Slaughter set her down on the plank sidewalk, but did not step back. She moved away from him, staring up into his face with a half pout, half smile. He was handsome, there was no denying that, with his blond, leonine mane, his chill, demanding eyes, and thin, expressive lips, the deep cleft in his chin. *If you were only a little different, Bob, she thought. And if only there weren't Paul. And if only a dozen other things,* she concluded bitterly, drawing a deep breath and turning into the Oxbow.

The barkeep looked up in surprise, but she gave him no heed. She had been doing a man's work with the Pickle Bar too long to worry about the dubious impropriety of her presence in a place like this. Kettle Cory sprawled in a chair against the wall, a tall bottle of red bourbon on the table before him, half empty. He was a prodigious man, with a great kettle gut that was always forcing the tails of his red wool shirt out of his belt with its insistent, beefy rolls of fat. Gail had never seen him when he wasn't sweating. Perspiration rolled like tears from the veined, dissolute pouches of his little eyes, gathering in rivulets along the deep grooves formed by his ruddy, unshaven jowls, and seeping greasily into the clefts and crevices of his assortment of chins. He was dozing placidly, with his fat hands folded across his paunch, and his muddy high-heeled boots spread out wide.

"Kettle," said Slaughter, shaking him.

The man opened his eyes without moving. They held a blue, lucid clarity that constantly surprised Gail in such a gross beast. "You don't need to shake me," said Kettle through pouted lips. "I know you're here, Slaughter."

"Come back to camp, Kettle," Gail told him. "We'll get a decent cook. I want to move out of here by morning."

"Let me kill this soldier," said Kettle. "I'll be there when you need me."

"You're coming now," said Slaughter, grabbing the man again.

"I said you didn't need to shake me, Bob," said Kettle without raising his voice.

Gail saw the flush filling Slaughter's face, and she put a hand on his arm, dragging it back. "All right, Kettle," she said. "I know you'll be there. Where are the others?"

"Couple of them wandered in here," said Kettle. "Then Windy showed up with word they'd found a good place to eat. Cowman's Rest, or something. Across the street."

"All right, Kettle," Gail told him. "I'm counting on you." She kept that hold on Slaughter, pulling him out through the doors with her and turning to go across the

24

street. "Why do the other men always leave him alone, Bob?"

"He's one of the best all-around hands I've ever seen," said Slaughter. "But he used to be a cattle inspector for the San Antonio Cattlemen's Association. You won't find many cowhands who cotton to those Association detectives."

"But he isn't with the SACA now," she said.

Slaughter shrugged. "The taint still remains. His personality don't help. As long as he does the work, that's all I care."

They waded through the boggy mud of the street to the café. Solo Sam was sitting disconsolately on the curbing, holding his jaw.

"I think he busted every bone below my teeth," he mumbled. "You aren't going in, are you?"

"Who busted?" said Slaughter.

"Pothooks Marrs," said Sam. "The coosie in there, the belly cheater. He's got the rest of the gang trapped and won't let them go."

"Trapped?" Gail wheeled angrily into the open door. It was ominously quiet in the single, large room. There were half a dozen round tables at one side, but they weren't occupied. It seemed to Gail that her whole crew was sitting on the long-legged stools at the counter. Like a bunch of dry dogies staring at water beyond a fence, their attention was fixed almost painfully on the man standing beside a steaming griddle.

He was built along the lines of a bull. Not the gaunt, cat-backed, rangy Texas longhorn variety, with all the beef melted from them by years of running the brush. More like a surly, shortened Angus breeder that had wallowed too long in a rich pasture, sleek all over with too much tallow on his hips and ribs, but giving the sense of coiled, potent muscle beneath that tallow with every motion he made. He even kept his head lowered like a ringy bull. His curly, dark-brown hair was thinning at the back of his head, and his neck was so thick, a roll of leathery flesh pinched out over his dirty white collar every time he lifted his head slightly.

"Listen to them *frijoles* simmer," said *Don* Vargas wonderingly. "Just like they used to sound in Juárez. I hope you're not cooking them *gringo* style. The Mexican way is the only way. Nobody in the world can cook like the Mexicans. You take *aves rellenas adobadas y asadas*. What on heaven and earth compares with that? You got to know how to wilt the onions, though. If the onions, they are not wilted right, the whole thing, she is spoil. The longer you cook them, the better they are. And the chile. *Ay, qué delicioso.* You break off the stems and roast the pods and steam them until they are tender, then you peel the meat away from the skins . . ."

"I'll cook the food," said the cook without turning around. "You eat it."

"*Por supuesto*, of course, *Señor* Pothooks," said *Don* Vargas placatingly. "I was just telling you . . ."

"You better not tell him anything, unless you want to git thrown out like Solo Sam," said Windy. "I never seen anybody like this since Pecos Bill. Did you ever hear about the time Bill got engaged to Slue Foot Sue? She insisted on riding Bill's horse, Widow Maker. Now, she knew nobody else but Bill could ride that bronc', but no horse had ever throwed her, either, so . . ."

"Will you shut up," said Waco Garrett. "Them beans is boiling over, Pothooks."

"Yeah," grumbled Pata Pala, "if you don't serve those steaks soon, they'll start sprouting legs again and . . ."

"I told you I'd do the cooking!" roared Pothooks.

Pata Pala reared up so hard his stool went from beneath him and the only thing that kept him from falling with it was his quick backward thrust of hips that slammed his good foot and the end of his peg leg onto the floor. Only then did Gail see what had caused him to jump like that. Where a moment before nothing but the bare wood of the counter had been, the blade of a big meat chopper was now buried. Pata Pala had been sitting with both hands flat on the counter, about three inches apart, and it must have struck directly between them. It was made from an old machete that had been broken off halfway down to the hilt, leaving about six inches of the broad, wicked blade, looking like a broad-bladed hatchet.

Gail could not believe the cook had thrown it without looking, but she had not seen him turn, and now he was bent over the steaks on the griddle, rolling them in batter one by one to pop in the oven. She realized how deceptive that look of tallow was on his body. Soft living may have put a little weight on his frame, but the swift, competent movements of his hands and arms, rolling those steaks, sent little ripples of thick and potent muscle up and down his back, beneath the worn denim shirt. An utter silence had settled over the room. Windy's mouth was still open. The scrape of Pata Pala's stool was startling as he dragged it back between his legs. Gail could not believe the man's violence alone held them in this awed silence. All of Slaughter's blows had never subdued them to this point. Then she saw the dirty plates before each one.

"If you're going to stay," whispered Solo Sam, thrusting his bruised jaw hesitantly through the door behind Gail, "try and fix it up so I can get another one of them steaks, too, hey?"

The hissing whisper, in that dead silence, turned the cook around, and Gail saw his face for the first time. It was as square-framed as his body. His cheek bones were broad and flat, with faint hollows beneath, into which crept the bluish sheen of his freshly shaved beard. His black brows were heavy and shaggy and low over his eyes, giving them a deep-socketed, withdrawing look. Those eyes matched the sullen dip of that head, heavy-lidded, somnolent, filled with a dark, smoldering violence that was veiled very poorly. He had a small dark mustache, and his lips did not move too much around the words.

"If you're eating, sit down. I'll get to you in a moment."

Gail glanced wryly at Slaughter, moved to the end of the counter, seating herself by Windy. The humor fled from the cook's face as soon as he turned back to his cooking. She saw him look out the window toward the Oxbow Saloon across the street. His chin sank against his neck, and whitened creases dug into the bluish tint of his jaw. There was a look of great tension to it, and Gail found herself looking across toward the Oxbow, wondering what he was staring at. But she could see nothing. When she looked back, Marrs had dropped his gaze and was busy forking the steaks onto plates.

With the feeling of some tense undercurrent moving through the café, she said to Windy in a low voice: "What's going on? I've never seen anybody hornswoggle the bunch of you like this before."

"He can throw all the knives in the place," said Windy, "as long as he keeps on cooking them steaks. Ain't a one of us'd do anything to jeopardize this next batch coming up. You saw old pegleg. After a month of that last biscuit-shooter, he'd crawl under a snake if it'd keep this kind of food coming our way. Pothooks Marrs, this cookie calls himself. That's what Solo Sam got throwed out for. He started asking too many personal questions about the name."

Gail found her eyes on Marrs's hands, moving with casual skill at his tasks, never a wasted motion. They were square and competent-looking, with a faint fuzz of curly black hairs covering their sinewy backs. She had not realized the significance of the scars, at first. Now she saw that they were not the marks a man would get at the stove. Gail had lived among cowhands too long to be mistaken about rope burns. There were no fresh ones, but they would mark him for life. He served Gail's crew, and then came down to her, wiping his hands on a dirty apron.

"How long since you rolled biscuits on a chuck wagon?" she asked.

He stopped wiping his hands, and for a moment there was a strange, poignant, almost stricken look in his eyes. Then that was obliterated by a sullen, angry defiance, and those heavy, bluish lids closed over his eyes till they were almost invisible. "I never cooked on a chuck wagon," he said.

"You ate at one," she said.

"Any man who hasn't, shouldn't be in Texas," he said. "What's it to you?"

"Take it easy, belly cheater," said Slaughter. "The lady is interested in cooks right now. We're the Pickle Bar and we just lost our coosie."

"How much do you make here?" said Gail.

"If you came in to eat," said Marrs, "give me your order. If you came in to ask questions, there's an information booth down in the Texas Pacific station for that very purpose."

Slaughter started to bend across the counter, but Gail caught him by a shoulder. "All right. I won't ask questions. I don't care what you make. I'll double it, if you can keep my crew this happy as far north as Dodge City. I'll even give you a bonus if you go the whole way with us."

"I'm happy here," said Marrs. "There's plenty of cooks around."

"Not range cooks, and you know it," she said. "They're as scarce as black spots on albinos."

"When you find a black spot, send me a letter," he said. "Do you want something to eat or don't you?"

"She wants you to answer a civil question," said Slaughter, kicking his stool back from under him, and

30

this time Gail couldn't stop his lunge across the counter. He caught the front of Marrs's shirt and jerked him across the planking, starting to yell in his face. "Now, tell the lady . . ."

It happened so fast after that Gail could not quite follow it. She heard the rip of cloth and saw Slaughter's hand in mid-air with a handful of white cotton. Then Slaughter was staggering backward and Gail realized Marrs must have hit him in the face. Marrs didn't stop with that. He grabbed a dishpan full of dirty china from under the counter and heaved the whole thing across the top at Slaughter. The trail boss was still staggering across the room, and had just been stopped by a table, when the dishpan and crockery struck him with a deafening *clatter*. He went backward over the table with the tin and china raining down over him and onto the floor, and the table collapsed, too.

"Now get out, damn you!" roared Marrs, whipping around to get a pot of boiling water and throwing it, pot and all, at the other men. "All of you, get out! Vamoose! Take a *pasear!* Empty the wagon . . ."

Howling with the boiling water in his face, Windy ducked the pot itself, and it *clanged* against the far wall. Then clean china began to rain down on them, and cutlery, and a dozen stools toppled as the crew made for the door, hands over their heads.

Pata Pala was the only one who even tried to fight back. He grabbed that machete from where it had still been buried in the counter, and started running down toward the end. Marrs vaulted the counter and caught the peg-legged man right there. Pata Pala came down with the flat of the blade at Marrs's head. The cook dodged in under it and struck Pata Pala's waist, knocking him back with such force that the man staggered clear back out into the street and fell in the mud.

Slaughter was starting to rise up from the wreckage across the room. He was still too dazed to do much but make a feeble pass as Marrs caught him by the belt, swinging him around, and shoving him toward the door. Slaughter tried to catch the doorframe and stop himself. Marrs scooped up a chair and threw it at him. It knocked the trail boss out across the sidewalk to fall on the peg-legged man just as Pata Pala started to rise. Snorting through flared, fluttering nostrils, making guttural animal sounds deep down in that thick throat, Marrs swept the curly hair off his forehead with a vicious motion of one hand, wheeling back toward the counter. He must have forgotten Gail, for he stopped, unable to hide the surprise.

"Aren't you going to throw me out, too?" she said, drawing herself up high and trying to fill with cold contempt.

"Lady," he said, standing spread-legged in the middle of the carnage, "if you don't go on your own two feet, right now, I sure will, very happily."

She stared at him for a moment. The humor of the whole thing had been pushing insistently upward in her since it started, and finally she could hold it down no longer. She lifted her chin to laugh.

"I have no doubt that you would," she said, and walked with as much dignity as she could summon to the door, turning there. "But don't forget, that offer still holds, twice what you're getting here, and a bonus. Our bed grounds are on the river south of town. Pickle Bar. Gail Butler."

"Get out!"

As she turned to step out on the sidewalk, she saw that Slaughter was getting to his feet. Some of the crockery in the dishpan must have hit him on the head, for he was reeling dazedly.

"I'll go back in there and tear him apart."

"Slaughter," Gail said sharply. "You stay out here."

"I'll kill him, I swear it!"

"If you go back in there, you're fired!"

The tone of her voice checked him. He halted at the curb, swaying, blinking. She stepped in front of him, blocking him off from the door.

"You're too good a cattleman to take that seriously," she said. "You riled a cook and you deserved what you got, all of you. You certainly won't lose any face with the crew by taking it. In fact, they'd begin to wonder what kind of a cowman you were if you did go back for revenge."

Her argument held logic that only a cattleman could appreciate. And Slaughter was still too dazed to hold much rage. He threw the long blond hair from his eyes with a toss of his head, glancing sullenly at the crew for affirmation.

"Gail's right, Slaughter." Solo Sam grinned. "Any cook with that much sand in his craw deserves to be let alone. He makes our last belly cheater look like a sop-and-tatters."

Slaughter rumbled deep in his chest. "If it was anybody but a cook, I'd kill him, I swear it."

"All right," Gail said, catching his elbow. "Let's go back to camp."

As they walked toward their horses, Windy shook his head. "A cook ain't really worth his biscuits unless he's ringy. But I never saw one *that* ringy."

"You must have touched him on a sore spot," *Don* Vargas told Gail. "If he punched cows, it was 'way back. He must have a good reason to keep him away from it that long. A lot of men with reasons that good are a little touchy about them."

"He won't show up on our outfit, that's sure," said Solo Sam.

"He'd better not," said Slaughter viciously.

Gail was looking back toward the Cowman's Rest. In her mind was a picture of that indefinable poignancy in Marrs's eyes when she had mentioned the range and the chuck wagon, like the almost unbearable nostalgia of an exile upon mention of his homeland — before the sullen suspicion had lowered the heavy lids over it, hiding it.

"On the contrary," she said. "Somehow, I think he will show up."

CHAPTER
FOUR

Thick, gray ground fog filled the hollows and crossed the higher flats like languid serpents when Gail peered out of the wagon at 5:00 the next morning. Already the cows were lowing disconsolately on their bed ground, and someone was puttering about the chuck wagon. She saw Windy's white head of hair. Slipping into a faded crinoline dress, she took the pins from her hair, and started combing it out, looking down at Paul beside her in the bed they had made in the linchpin.

His face looked even weaker in sleep. The relaxation of facial muscles dropped his mouth open, allowing his undershot jaw to recede into the sallow folds of flesh forming his neck. It seemed to epitomize the weakness she had come to see in him so clearly these last years. She found a strange, vagrant thought in her head. How would Pothooks Marrs breathe in his sleep?

It almost made her laugh. What a crazy thing to think! She tossed her taffy hair, sighed deeply, climbed out over the tailgate, and walked through the damp grass to the chuck wagon.

"Thought I'd get a few things ready for you," Windy told her. "Fires lit. Dutch ovens are hot. This ain't going to be no picnic, Miss Gail, trying to cook for them rannihans."

"I'm sure they won't dump me in the river if I burn the steak," she said. "Anyway, it's just till I can hunt up a cook. Did you get someone to cut out a steer for meat?"

"The Caverango Kid is saddling up," said Windy disgustedly. "He's so eager to graduate off the cavvy he'd rope a locomotive if you asked him."

"How many times have you told me you started by wrangling horses for the Big Skillet?" she chided him.

Windy shrugged, making unintelligible noises that moved his Adam's apple up and down in his scrawny neck. Then the voice of *Don* Vargas floated around the chuck wagon.

"Now why don't you take my advice and use this rawhide *reata*, Kid? Look how supple she is. So narrow the wind don't affect her at all. You want to be a good roper, don't you? Only the best use rawhide."

"And when twelve hundred pounds of beef hits the other end, the rawhide comes apart like hot molasses," said the Kid.

"Nothing breaks if you dally," said *Don* Vargas in a hurt tone.

"They wouldn't let me back in Texas if they found me taking turns around my horn."

"*¡Sacramento!*" exploded *Don* Vargas. "You *Tejanos* think the only way to rope is to tie it so hard on your horn a herd of buffalo couldn't pull it off. What happens if the bull bounces back up and goes for you?

36

I've seen more than one tie-hard man gored to death because he couldn't let go his rope quick enough."

The Kid must have been tugging at his latigo, because the words came out in a series of grunts: "Any roper bad enough to let that happen deserves whatever he gets."

"*Buey, buey,*" spat *Don* Vargas. "Just wait a minute. I'm going out with you right now and prove how much better a rawhide *reata* is than your stupid sisal clothesline. You don't know what roping is till you've seen a real Mexican *vaquero* toss a hide string."

"Doesn't the *don* ever give up?" said Gail, dumping a whole pound package of Triple X into the coffee pot.

Windy emitted a snorting laugh. "He's been telling me how superior those Mexican cactus tree saddles is to our Porter rigs all the way from Austin. Last rain we came through got his tree so wet the cactus wood turned to pulp and his whole saddle just sort of melted out from beneath him while he was sitting right in it. I never saw a man look so . . . so . . ." Windy broke off, looking past her, and that Adam's apple began to bob up and down, and she knew what was coming out. "Well, eat all my blackstrap, if we ain't got a cook!"

Gail turned to see Pothooks Marrs riding up out of the river bottom. It was an old whey-bellied mare he rode, but there was a cattle brand on its right hip, and it still tried to pick up its hoofs like it had cut a pretty thin biscuit in its prime. Marrs had on an old canvas Mackinaw with his hands stuffed in his pockets, and a disreputable flat-topped horse-thief hat jammed down so low on his head it almost hid his eyes. The bridle reins were tied and slung on the horn, and he didn't even bother taking his hands from his pockets when he dismounted. Gail knew the animal had been a roper then, for it halted sharply as soon as Marrs swung his right leg over the cantle to step off. On the ground he turned and unlashed a war bag from behind the battered old Porter saddle, and without a word walked over to the chuck wagon and heaved the bag through the pucker in front. Then he came back and faced Gail.

"I was drawing down fifty a month at the Cowman's Rest," he said.

"A hundred dollars is a lot for a cook," she said. "But I gave you my word. A couple of the boys will be in with a steer for steaks in a few minutes. I've got the Triple X boiling."

Their talking had finally roused others in the crew. Solo Sam thrust his long, sleepy face over the lip of his sougan and, when he saw who it was, let out a wild Rebel yell that brought the others bouncing out of their blankets and grabbing for guns. They crowded around Marrs, clapping him on the back and laughing like a bunch of schoolboys. He took it all indifferently, shoving them off like a patient dog tolerating a bunch of children, but they would not leave him alone, and at last Gail saw a flitting smile part his lips, revealing startling white teeth beneath that little mustache. Then, abruptly, all the good-natured raillery ceased. Bob Slaughter had appeared.

He must have been down at the river, sousing his head, for his long yellow hair was streaming down his face. He shoved it back with an impatient palm, striding in that long-legged way through the men toward Marrs. Gail drew in a sharp breath, stepping toward him, but he reached Marrs before she could stop him.

"You got a lot of gall coming out here after yesterday," he told Marrs.

"You take it too personally," said Marrs. "You should know better than to rile a cook. Missus Butler's hired me, Slaughter, and I'll tell you right now, boss or no boss, the same thing will happen again any time you poke your nose in my kitchen. I'll tend to my cooking and you tend to your cows and everybody'll be happy."

Slaughter's grin flattened his lips against his teeth in a cold, mirthless way. "The other cooks had the same ideas, Marrs. That's why I'm not going to bother to take it personally. You'll dig your own grave. I don't think you'll measure up to this crew's standards for a biscuit-shooter. They may welcome you like a long lost brother now, but that's because they haven't eaten decent food in a week. Wait till we run into a sandstorm and you get your pie full of gravel. It isn't the same as cooking inside a nice dry room. Wait till it rains too hard for fires and they have to eat jerky and dried apples three or four days straight. You'll wish to hell you were back in Dallas at a tenth the salary you're getting now. I'll give you two weeks, Marrs. And that's stretching wet rawhide."

Marrs gazed at him without speaking for a moment. He reminded Gail of a sulking bull again, withdrawn so deeply into himself, needing only a spark to set off an explosion. But for all the sense of latent violence, when he spoke, his voice was soft as silk. And it wasn't to Slaughter that he spoke. He turned his back on the man and told Gail: "I'll start out with the sourdough keg."

"Last cook kept it under the seat," Solo Sam said. "I'll fetch it for you . . ."

"Don't touch it!"

Marrs's voice held all the lash of a whip. It checked Sam halfway to the chuck wagon. He turned around, eyes wide with surprise. Marrs walked past him to the wagon, hoisting himself up onto a wheel, lifting the five-gallon keg from beneath the seat. He looked at it disgustedly.

"How did he expect the dough to work if he didn't keep it warm? How about somebody's extra saddle blanket?"

The crew stared at him wonderingly. Then Solo Sam turned to walk over to the scattered sougans, rummaging through his till he came up with a tattered blanket. He brought it to Marrs, and the cook wrapped it carefully around the keg. Then he took off the top, sniffed, put his ear inside the keg.

"Not even fermenting," he muttered. "How about some blackstrap?"

Gail rattled around behind the shelves till she found the jug of molasses. Marrs took it up by its long black strap and measured it carefully into the sourdough.

"Now," he said, almost as if talking to himself, "sun comes out, that dough'll start working. You must have had a stable boy for a cook."

"Have to admit his bread was a little flat," Sam said.

"All right." Marrs slapped the keg, turning to them. "As long as I'm rattling the pans here, I don't want anybody to touch this keg. I find a man with his hands on it, he's going to get the nearest pot of hot grease dumped down his neck."

"That's taking a lot on your shoulders, Marrs," Slaughter said.

Marrs turned to him. "You want a cook, or don't you?"

Windy cackled. "I'd put up with it, Slaughter. The only good cooks I ever knew thought more of their sourdough keg than they did their Bible. I knew one that got so sentimental over his keg he had the parson tie it to him in holy wedlock."

Before Slaughter could answer, a shout caused them to turn westward. The Caverango Kid and *Don* Vargas were hazing a big steer the color of mulberries away from the fringe of the herd and toward the chuck wagon. The Kid was swinging his sisal rope around his head.

"I told you, *Tejanos* didn't know how to rope!" bawled the Mexican. "You'll scare every cow off the bed ground swinging that community loop on top, Kid. Watch a real roper."

"Let's not have any rodeo!" Marrs shouted at them. "Just set the steer down here and leave your fancy work for the grandstand."

"*¡Viva!*" cried *Don* Vargas, and made his bid in an underhanded dab that flirted the light, supple rawhide out toward the steer's forelegs. But the steer veered and put its head into the loop.

41

"Is that the way they do it in Mexico?" jeered Windy.

Crestfallen, *Don* Vargas spurred his horse in to get slack, but Marrs called to him in an angry voice. "Leave it on his neck. I don't care how you throw him, just get him down. Heel him, Kid, and stretch him out."

With an eager whoop, the Kid raced in at the rear of the bull, tossing for the kicking hind legs. Windy held his nose at this poor show. Any Texan considered it beneath him to team-rope a steer. Just as the Caverango Kid made his throw, the steer wheeled sharply. This caused its full weight to hit the end of *Don* Vargas's rope anew.

There was the *squeal* of hot rawhide as the dallies slid on the Mexican's flat-topped horn. But even this did not provide enough give. The *pop* was sharp as a gunshot, and the steer somersaulted with the broken end of the rawhide rope flaying empty air.

"Let him go, Kid!" shouted Solo Sam.

But the Kid's loop was already out, catching those heels as they came up from the somersault. He had a short rope and it was tied hard and he was still running in the direction he had turned when he expected *Don* Vargas's rope to be on the other end. He tried to rein away so the weight wouldn't hit the end of his rope with the horse still broadside. The horse changed leads to wheel, and a thousand pounds of beef hit the end of the rope right there, with the horse completely off balance. Gail heard the sick sound Windy made as all four feet went from beneath the horse.

With a scared shout, the Kid tried to kick free of his stirrups. His left leg was still beneath the horse when it hit. With slack in the rope, the dazed steer scrambled free of the loop and lunged to its feet. The frightened, whinnying horse did the same thing. Then Gail saw why the Kid hadn't gotten that other leg free. His heel had broken off and his foot had slipped through the stirrup.

"Get him!" she screamed, running toward the horse. "Get him somebody, he'll be dragged!"

This only frightened the horse more, and it spun and bolted in the direction of the wagons. The other men all started going after it, but it was the cook's movement that caught Gail's attention. She did not think she had ever seen a man move so fast. Instead of going directly after the horse, Marrs spun and ran in quick, stabbing little steps to the sougans scattered over the grounds. Most of the men used their own saddles for pillows, and he bent over, without lessening his driving run, to rip a rope off one of the rigs. His run had quartered him away from the animal so that he was now out at one side of it, while the other men were still bunched directly in behind the beast. But it was obvious they could never catch it, and Pata Pala had already veered off to get a horse.

The running animal had almost reached the chuck wagon, dragging the Kid, his head banging from side to side on the ground, his arms flailing — and Gail knew the boy would be killed if the horse ever got past the wagon, with the whole prairie to run in. It was only Marrs, in that last moment, who held the Kid's life in his hands.

He did it casually, with no sense of crisis to the thing. Still running, he flirted the loop out and made the toss in an underhanded swipe that came straight out of the Texas brush.

"Oh, no!" sobbed Gail, because the horse was running to go behind the chuck wagon, and, by the time that rope reached him, there would be no more than a foot between the hind wheel and the front of the horse, and the loop was too big to go in front of the animal without fouling up on the wheel. Gail stopped running, sinking to one knee in hopeless despair as that swinging loop sped after the horse. Then, although she could not really believe it, she realized that the loop was growing smaller as it flew, the hondo was sliding down the rope even as Marrs paid it out. At the finish, it was no bigger than the top of a Stetson.

It still would have struck the wheel, but in the last instant Marrs flirted his downpointed hand upward, and the loop stood on end, and went between horse and wagon wheel like a rolling hoop. The horse put his forefeet right into it. Marrs wheeled away with the rope across one hip, and his whole body jerked as the animal went down. Gail still remained on that one knee, dazed, unable to believe it possible. The other men had run up, and Solo Sam sat on the horse's head while Windy disentangled the Kid's foot. Blood covered the boy's face, but Gail got a pail of water from the butt and one of the clean dishrags, washing it away, and saw that the cuts were not bad. He was not completely unconscious, and, when he had recovered somewhat from his daze, he just sat there, staring up at Marrs, holding his head in his hands.

"I didn't get it all," he muttered. "I only know there wasn't enough room between the wagon and that horse to stick a Barlow knife in. I didn't even look for it to come from you. How did you get a rope on him?"

Marrs shrugged. "Never had any more room than that down . . ." He caught himself up, and Gail looked at him.

"Down where, Pothooks?"

She saw that sullen withdrawal lower the heavy sensuous lids over his dark eyes till they were barely visible. "Never mind."

"But we will mind," said Slaughter, something mocking in the laughing tone of his voice. "Looks like brush country roping to me. Is that what you mean, Marrs? Down in the brush. What are you doing so far north . . . ?"

"I said never mind," Marrs told him in a sharp, guttural tone.

"Reminds me of the time Pecos Bill lost his horse across the river." Windy chuckled. "It was spring flood and bank full and too dangerous for him to swim, but he was afraid the animal would wander off over there if he didn't stake him. So he tied six ropes together till he had about three hundred and fifty feet of line, and . . ."

"Put your jaw in a sling, you're liable to step on it," growled Pata Pala.

"If somebody don't get me that steer," said Marrs, "all you'll eat for breakfast is whistle berries and Texas butter, and not much of that."

Solo Sam got a rope and walked out toward the remuda for his horse. Marrs went around to the fires and began stirring them up. Gail made sure the boy was all right, getting some kerosene and lard from the drawer behind the chuck wagon to put on those cuts and bruises. Sam brought in his pied bronco and slung on a kak and then went out after the blue steer again. While he and Windy were throwing and killing and butchering it, Gail watched Marrs make his bread. She found her eyes on the casual competence of those square, hairy, rope-scarred hands again, as he rolled the dough out for light bread, shaping it in pans, and slipping the pans into a Dutch oven. The lid of the oven had been previously heated, and on the top of it he put several more shovels full of coal. Windy brought him a hindquarter of the yearling, and Marrs cut many thin steaks about the size of his palm from it. These he rolled in the flour left from the bread making, and dropped into another Dutch oven, which already held about three inches of crackling, red-hot lard. When these steaks were finished, Gail got three or four of them, covered with crisp, delicious brown batter, for herself and Paul, and, putting tin cups of coffee and pan bread on the tray, carried it to him. He was awake and stirring restlessly.

"It's about time you got here," he said. "What's held you up? This bread is soggy."

"It was too dry yesterday," she told him. "You're getting peevish in the wagon, Paul. You haven't any fever today. Why don't you get out a little bit?"

"And catch my death of cold," he said. "You know I'm not well yet, Gail. Why do you always prod me to get out?" The whites of his eyes had a yellowish tinge in the gloom, sliding up to her. "Maybe you want me to get sick, is that it?"

"Oh, stop it, Paul."

"You and Slaughter must be having a good time, out riding the herd with him every day, going into town . . ."

"I had to go into town. We needed a new cook."

"And at Corsicana you needed some flour," he said. "I know, Gail, I know, a sick man doesn't please you very much, does he? A nice, healthy young woman like you needs a hand with some vinegar in his blood . . ."

"Paul, will you stop it," she said. "It's not that and you know it."

"What is it, then?" He studied her narrowly. "You'd do it if I was well anyway. Is that it?"

"Do what?" she said thinly.

He grimaced at the coffee. "You said a new cook? More like a crazy-wagon belly cheater with this sheep dip."

"It's the best coffee you've had in months and you know it."

"How ardent you are in his defense," he murmured. "Perhaps the cook is handsome, too."

"Paul, will you stop it, please." She turned away, on the verge of tears. "Why does it have to be like this? All the time. You're getting morbid in here, Paul. Won't you please get out, just a little bit?"

"No. Will you stop asking me that? No!" He swept his food off the tray with a vicious motion, dropping heavily back into the blankets. "Take it out. It's foul. Get me something decent to eat."

She remained on her knees, staring dully at him. Then she started gathering it up. She made no sound, but she could not stop the tears from gathering in her eyes. She tried to turn her face away before he saw the first one cross her cheek. But he must have caught it. She heard him stirring at her side, and tensed for another tirade. Instead, she felt his hand on her arm, turning her around, and she was pulled against him.

"Gail, honey, I'm sorry, forgive me. Gail?" His hands were molding her shoulder, her neck, caressing her hair tenderly, deftly. "I don't know what makes me like this. It is the confinement, I guess. Forgive me. I'm a fool."

Her face was against his chest, where she had found such comfort before, after their battles. But now she could gain no assurance from his contrition. The hands were too deft, stroking her head. It had happened too many times before.

"Why do we have to be this way, Paul?" she said in a choked, tortured whisper. "We never used to quarrel."

"I don't know, Gail," he said. "It's my fault. This sickness. This worrying over the Pickle Bar. Forgive me, honey."

She drew a heavy, resigned breath. "Yes, Paul."

He emitted a small laugh, settling back. "That's better. No reason for us to quarrel. Tell me about the new cook."

"Not much to tell." She started gathering up the stuff once more. "He's rather reserved. He's a good roper."

"Roper?"

"Yes." She looked up, staring blankly at the hoops of the wagon, as it was brought to her mind again. "In fact, Paul, he's probably the best roper I've ever seen. Did you ever see a man throw a hooley-ann clear to the end of a rope, Paul?"

He shrugged. "That isn't so rare. Any top hand can do it. I've seen Waco pull it in a corral."

"But not put a mangana in it at the same time," she said. "If Waco can hit a mangana, it's got to be a community loop at half that distance, and even then he misses one out of two. But Pothooks was throwing a hooley-ann, Paul. The loop wasn't any bigger than the crown of your hat when it hit the end of that rope, and he stood it on end in the neatest mangana you ever saw. That horse stepped right into it."

Paul let out a rueful laugh. "All right, all right, don't get so excited about it. So he's a grandstander."

"No," she said. "It couldn't have been done any other way. He saved the Kid's life." She turned to him, a plate in her hand. "Paul, he isn't a grandstander. He isn't the type. He didn't want to do that. I saw it in him, just that instant before he went for the rope, just a moment there, when he had to choose between revealing how good he was with a clothesline or letting the Kid die."

Paul was interested now, frowning at her. "You mean he's *that* good?"

"I told you, Paul," she said. "I never saw anything like it. A man like that doesn't come along often. Pothooks Marrs. Does the name mean anything to you? Pretty far back, probably. Those rope marks on his hands are old. Ten, fifteen years. Down in the brush country. A short, heavy-set man with eyes like a sulking bull and a little black mustache and very white teeth."

"Pothooks Marrs." Paul said it speculatively, sucking in his lower lip. He shook his head faintly. "No. It doesn't do anything to me. You mean he has a past?"

"All the signs point that way," she said.

He shrugged again. "Well, so what? Half the men you run into along the trail have a past. I think Solo Sam is riding from something. Slaughter himself has buried a lot of dirty bones in his time."

"But not like this," she said. "Not so afraid of revealing themselves that they'd take another job. That would be the worst kind of torture for a man with cattle in his blood. Maybe this isn't his real name. Can't you think of someone, Paul? Someone so good at his trade he can't work at it for fear his skill would mark him."

"They don't come that good very often, Gail. You know it. Quite a few men dropped out of sight down San Antonio way during that time. Ten years ago? You know how rough it was. Gardin Barrett was awfully good on the rope. But he was a big lanky man." He halted so sharply she bent toward him. "M . . . Marrs," he said. His eyes narrowed. "Lee M. Benton. Could that be it? Nobody ever did know what the M was for." He shook his head abruptly. "No. It couldn't be."

"Who was Lee M. Benton?" she said.

50

"Never mind. It couldn't be him."

"Who was he?" she insisted.

"I told you never mind," he snarled. "You wouldn't want to know."

"Paul." She could not help the ominous little catch in her voice. "Why wouldn't I want to know?"

CHAPTER
FIVE

One thousand three- and four-year-olds with the elongated Pickle Bar on their gaunt, dusty rumps strung out up the bottom land of the Trinity toward Denison and Colbert's Ferry and Fort Sill and Dodge. The dust they raised formed a haze that sometimes obscured the sun, and their hoarse bawling formed a constant undertone to the intermittent shout of a drag rider or a pointer. On the tail end, a ghostly, rocking figure in the dust, rode Solo Sam, singing "That Dad Blame Boss" in his dubious baritone:

> *I'll get me a new slicker*
> *And some Coffeyville boots*
> *Buy a quart of good red likker,*
> *And quit this old galoot . . .*

At the chuck wagon, Pothooks Marrs had dumped the remaining hot water in the wreck pan full of dirty tin plates and cups, and was washing them. For a moment, the sounds of cattle and the dust and that off-key song lifted him out of his brooding, somber mood. He stared out across the dim, bobbing, long-horned heads, and took a deep, careful breath, like a man would take a deep draft of good liquor, savoring it. How long was it since he had been a part of this? He didn't like to recall. It was like a lost space in his life, a vacuum. It was strange how cattle remained in a man's blood. He had heard an old sailor try to explain the same thing about the sea once. If it got hold of you, there was no forgetting it. The pull of it would always be there, and sooner or later, if you lived long enough, you would go back.

Well, he was back. And it was good. He couldn't deny that. He could taste it; it was so good. It didn't matter why he had come back. It didn't matter that he was running from Kettle Cory, and all the rest, as he had been running for so long.

After Gail and the Pickle Bar crew had left yesterday afternoon, Marrs had remained in the Cowman's Rest, still unwilling to take the chance of Kettle's seeing him, apprehensive that the fight would draw the fat man over.

Marrs realized that the whole thing had been precipitated by his own immense tension, with Kettle waiting in the Oxbow like that. He was as ringy as the next cook, because that was tradition, and a man liked to be let alone at his trade, but he knew that, if he hadn't been so jumpy, he wouldn't have blown his top that way.

But it hadn't drawn Kettle over. And half an hour later, the fat man had left the Oxbow, three sheets to the wind, and had teetered on down Jackson, apparently in search of another saloon. When the man was out of sight, Marrs had left the café, over Bob

Warren's protest, and had gone to his room down on Poydras. His whole impulse had been flight, then. He couldn't stay in town with Kettle there. Maybe Kettle was hunting him, maybe not. It didn't matter. He had to leave.

But a man with $5 in his kick couldn't get very far. It was then that he remembered Gail Butler's offer. What better than to lose himself in the anonymity of a trail herd heading north? He decided, however, that it would be better to remain hidden in his room and go out in the morning just before the herd was ready to start. He had spent a sleepless night, watching the street below, and had gone to the livery for his old roping mare early this morning. And so now he was here, and he tried to bury his reasons for coming and let the exhilaration of the sights and sounds and smells run through him like a tonic.

But he couldn't bury his reasons. Because already they were cropping up. Why did it have to be that way? The first crack out of the box. But he'd had to do it. It had been the only way of saving the Kid's life, and he'd had to throw his rope. And it had put something in Gail's mind. He had seen the look on her face. Where did a cook learn to rope like that? Who would she ask first?

He looked up as the whinny of a high-stepping horse heralded the approach of the Caverango Kid, herding the cavvy of spare animals by. He reined in his bronco, greeting Marrs.

"How's the head?" asked the cook, without smiling.

54

"Fine, thanks to you." The Kid grinned. His horse pirouetted around, but the boy reined him back to look at Marrs once more, a strange, indefinable expression shining in his eyes.

"Better get on to your cavvy," Marrs said gruffly.

"Sure, Pothooks." There was worship in the boy's voice. He grinned down at the sourdough keg. "Looks like you used it for a pillow."

"Softest one in the world."

"Why do you put so much store in a little old keg?"

"Man ain't a good cook unless you see him taking his keg to bed with him. Lose anything else. Lose them circle mules, lose the Triple X, lose the spare horses. The crew'll still get along. But you lose that sourdough keg and an outfit is really in hard times. It might as well quit."

The Kid's eyes were wide with wonder. "Maybe you need another blanket for it. I got a spare."

"It's all right now. If it ain't working fast enough to suit, you an' me'll take turns setting on it, just like a hen."

The Kid laughed out loud, gave Marrs a last worshipful look, and spurred his horse after the cavvy. Marrs stared after him, letting the warmth seep slowly through him, savoring it. A man could only feel that way with the friendship of other men, and it was something he hadn't known in a long time.

Then Guy Bedar came around the front of the wagon, narrow, hatchet-faced, leading a horse as filthy as himself. The earth caked on its fetlocks looked like drying bottom mud.

"If Slaughter's right about you still having to make your peace with the crew, there's your first recruit," said Bedar, leaning against a wheel to roll himself a cigarette. He chuckled throatily. "It's funny about a kid, isn't it? First off, Slaughter was a little tin god. He couldn't do wrong. Caverango was going to be a trail boss and woo every filly from Doan's Crossing north and take Dodge apart with his bare hands at the end of every drive. He was bouncing around too much to get a good look at that job of roping you did, but they've all been feeding him full of it. He was out there this morning trying to put a mangana in a hooley-ann."

"He'll get over it," said Marrs heavily.

"You better hope not," said Bedar. "Come a time when you're going to need every friend you got in this outfit. And they don't exactly number in the thousands right now."

Now bent over the wreck pan, Marrs looked up abruptly. "What the hell are you hanging around for?"

"Slaughter told me to pilot you over the tough country northward," said Bedar. He took a deep drag on the cigarette, glanced over toward the linchpin. There was no sign of Gail, and he dropped the smoke, grinding it out with a heel. "Someone else also told me something. There's a man down in the brakes that would like to see you."

"He wants to see me, he can come up here," said Marrs, piling dishes into the chuck box.

"On the contrary," said Bedar. "You'd better go down there . . . Lee."

Marrs whirled so sharply it jerked a breath from him in a hoarse grunt. The blood had receded from his cheeks, leaving them pale. His nostrils fluttered faintly, like a spooked horse. When he spoke, it was barely audible.

"Bedar?" he said, frowning, searching the man's face.

The man laughed, tossing his head. "Oh, don't go hunting your back trails for me. I wasn't there. First time I laid eyes on you was this morning. But when I told Rickett about that roping, he knew who it was right away."

"Rickett!"

"Yeah," said Bedar. "Down in the brakes."

Marrs felt that old, hopeless sickness again. It seemed as if it was all coming down on him like an irrepressible weight. Could Rickett be with Kettle? But why this eternal game? If they wanted him, why didn't they come and get him? More and more he was seeing how it didn't fit. If they were really after him, they wouldn't send for him this way; they wouldn't tip him off and give him a chance to escape.

"What does Rickett want?" Marrs asked in a tight voice.

"Maybe he wants to make a deal," Bedar said.

"Is he still with the San Antonio Cattlemen's Association?"

Bedar smiled secretively. "He hasn't been with them for ten years. I know what you're worried about. It ain't that. Rickett can forget what happened down in Refugio County, if you see things his way." Bedar saw the intense anger fill Marrs's face, and said softly: "I'd

57

go down and talk to him, anyway, Pothooks. If you really want this cooking job, it would be too bad if Rickett had to come up here and maybe tell Gail Butler who you really are."

A whipped look came into Marrs's face. He walked around to the front of the wagon, climbing on a wheel to reach behind the seat for his war bag. From this he extracted a big Whitneyville Walker with most of the bluing worn off its long barrel. He thrust it in his belt right behind the buckle. Then he slung the ancient, rawhide-laced kak on his whey-bellied mare and unhitched her from the wagon, walking her back to where Bedar stood.

"Let's go," he said doggedly.

The mud along the bottoms had that same waxen gloss to it as the muck in the streets of Dallas. The animals sank to their fetlocks in some places, and every time they stopped, the mud relinquished their hoofs with sucking, chortling reluctance. Rickett was waiting in a bunch of scrub oak. He had the same facile mouth, thought Marrs, a little heavier about the jowls, the same eyes, pouched a little deeper by dissipation. Gray was beginning to tinge his temples. He bent forward slightly to stare at Marrs, a vague wonder filling his eyes.

"I'd expected a *little* change," he said in a low voice. "Not this much. I don't think I'd recognize you if I saw you on the street, Lee."

"What do you want?" said Marrs sullenly.

"Now don't be like that," said Rickett. "This is Thibodaux, Lee."

58

"Pothooks," corrected Marrs doggedly. He needed but one glance to read most of the story in the dark man with queued hair and the slender, pendant hands. "I asked you what you wanted, Rickett."

"I want to tell you about Ellsworth," said Rickett.

"You don't have to," said Marrs. "With the quarantine law extended west of town, it's easy enough to see Ellsworth is through as a cattle terminus. Is that who you're working for now, Rickett? All the boys on South Main? I do imagine it pays more than inspecting brands for the old Association."

A subtle alteration darkened those guileless blue eyes momentarily. Then Rickett shrugged. "It does at that. A lot of money in gambling, Lee . . . ah, pardon me, Pothooks. That is, if you're on the right side of the table. The interests I represent hate to lose that money. They will if the cattle don't hit Ellsworth this year. I tried to explain it to Slaughter. I tried to show him how a man of his caliber formed a greater example than he realized along the trail. If he busted through to Ellsworth, the others would follow. On the other hand, Dodge City isn't established yet, and, if he turned off on a new route in that direction, and a whole string of appalling accidents happened, preventing him from getting through, it would cause a lot of them to go to Ellsworth anyway. He's turning off toward Dodge at the Red. Those accidents are going to start happening right soon. You're going to cause a lot of them. You always were good at the head of a herd, Pothooks. The Red River's flooding hell over her banks. She's ripe for you to help Bedar get that herd of Pickle Bar's in a mill and drown as many as you can. Maybe that'll make Slaughter believe we mean what we say. If it don't, we have a lot more cards up our sleeve."

"You just dropped this one out," said Marrs. "I tell you it's no go."

"Did it ever strike you," said Rickett blandly, "how many men would like to see you dead?"

There was no sound for a moment after that. They stared at each other without speaking. A horse snorted dismally. Finally Rickett laughed harshly.

"I guess you know that about as well as anyone," he said. "I guess it's why you stayed so low after you got out of jail. They didn't think they were dealing with such a dangerous man when they chose you, did they? They thought you were just a simple little maverick to hang a bell on."

Marrs made a spasmodic, impatient move to one side, as if to wheel his horse, but Rickett held up his hand. "That's just what I mean, Pothooks. Were you planning on leaving the Pickle Bar now? How useless it would be to try and skip again. All I'd have to do is drop the word that I'd seen Lee Marrs Benton. You couldn't change your appearance so radically again. Age did most of it for you. And there's hardly a place you could run that they wouldn't be. Boa Snyder and Curt Young are up in Montana now. Boa has the biggest outfit in the territory, runs a crew of a hundred men. If he heard you were back, and what you looked like, and what you were doing, you couldn't put your foot north of the Platte without him finding you. The Melbourne brothers are big shippers in Frisco, too. And

Dee Nation sits a fancy saddle in Webb County politics . . . a sheriff and a dozen town marshals to work for him, even a few Rangers to put on your track if he really tried hard."

Marrs stared at him another long space, the smoldering fire in his eyes growing brighter and brighter, and then, with a vicious jerk, he necked the mare in a wheeling turn. Rickett took one step forward, grabbing her bit before she could get all the way around.

"Hold up, Pothooks," he said. "I want your word on it. You're staying with the Pickle Bar. You know how useless it would be to run. And you're doing what I ask, all along."

"I am not!" It left Marrs in an explosive shout. He let Rickett's pull on the bit spin the mare back, and leaned out of the saddle toward the man, saying it in a guttural, shaken way: "I didn't come back looking for any blood, Rickett. I'm not bitter and I don't want revenge. I just want to be left alone. And, by God, if you don't leave me alone, I'll kill you."

"He said he'd kill me, Thibodaux," said Rickett.

"*C'est extraordinaire*," murmured the Creole.

"Let go, Rickett!" shouted Marrs.

"Don't get so high-handed," said Rickett, yanking the rearing mare back down. "You're in no position . . ."

"I said let me go!" roared Marrs, once more necking the mare, this time so hard that she spun in against Rickett, and booting her in the kidneys at the same time. She bolted forward, jerking Rickett off balance, and bringing him within range of Marrs's boot as he jerked his foot from the stirrup and lashed out at Rickett. It caught Rickett in the shoulder, tearing his grip off the bit, and the forward plunge of the horse spun him around on its barrel, back against Marrs's leg. Marrs kicked him away.

"Get him!" shouted Rickett, trying to keep from falling into the mud.

With the mare still bolting forward, Marrs saw what Thibodaux meant to do, and knew he was in no position to meet it with his own gun. He laid the reins on the right side of the mare's neck with a vicious jerk, and the horse veered sharply to the left, right at Thibodaux. The Creole had to forget about his gun and take a dive aside to keep from being struck by the charging beast.

Guy Bedar's cow pony must have had a take-off like a jack rabbit, because it lunged into Marrs's vision on his right side, head lifted high with the pain of the rider's big Petneckey spurs raking its flanks. It caught the mare a few feet beyond where Thibodaux had left it, and Bedar threw himself bodily off his horse at Marrs.

The man's weight carried Marrs off his mare, and they fell heavily into the mud. Marrs struck first, with Bedar's weight coming fully upon him to knock the breath out. Still, he managed to hook an arm about the man's neck and roll over on top. Then all that latent, smoldering violence fulfilled itself in the savage fist Marrs smashed in the man's face. Bedar made a sick sound, and went limp.

Marrs started getting onto his feet, but he was faced in such a direction that he caught a dim, blurred glimpse of Thibodaux rising from where he had dived into the mud, and of the man's intent. Knees still bent, Marrs whirled toward the Creole, yanking at the Walker Colt in his belt at the same time.

"Thibodaux!" shouted Rickett. "Hold it!"

Marrs stopped his own draw with the tip of the Colt's barrel still through his belt. What would have happened if he had pulled it on out was a certainty. Both men had started diving for iron at the same moment, but Thibodaux's gun had cleared its holster before Marrs even touched the handle of his Walker. Marrs would have finished the draw anyway, if Rickett hadn't shouted. But the chance that Thibodaux would obey Rickett was better than bucking certain death by going through with his draw.

Carefully Marrs straightened up, shoving the Colt slowly back into his belt. Thibodaux stood, holding his gun on Marrs with no expression in his sloe eyes. Rickett got up out of the mud, taking a futile swipe at the muck on his pants.

"Just had them cleaned, too, damn you," he said mildly. Then he looked up, as if seeing the scene in its entirety for the first time. "How do you like my boy? Did you ever see anybody so fast with a smoke pole?" He paused, as if expecting an answer. When Marrs made no sound, Rickett spoke to the Creole without looking in his direction: "You can put it away now, Thibodaux. I don't think the man is going to antagonize us any more. I think he knows what a tight chute he's in. I think he'll go back to the Pickle Bar and stay right there, in a prime position to do whatever we want, whenever we want. Don't you, Thibodaux?"

"Whatever we want," said Thibodaux.

CHAPTER
SIX

A chaparral bird burst from the prickly pear to run across an open space in the bottom lands, its plumage comically ruffled. Northward, clouds formed tiers on the horizon, darkening with the threat of rain, as somber as the mood filling Pothooks Marrs as he made his way back to the chuck wagon. A few hundred feet from where he had left Rickett and the others, something caught his eye. It was a bit of red cloth caught on a bush. Beneath it, the mud was trampled as if a horse had stood there for some time. Bending to scan the ground, he saw footprints leading away from the bush back in the direction from which he had come. It was all fresh sign, and could not logically come from any of the men he had seen. He picked the red patch off the bush, feeling its texture. Woolen. He stuffed it into a pocket and rode on.

In his mind, mostly, were Pickett's words: *There's hardly a place you could run that they wouldn't be.* For a moment the certainty of that filled him with a tenuous fear, a suffocated sense of constriction. How well Rickett had read him! He *had* meant to skip the Pickle Bar, to get out, to run. But Rickett's words only underlined the futility of that.

The only thing that had enabled Marrs to remain hidden up to now was the change in him. From a kid to a man, with all that added weight, and all the harrowing years in between. He had counted on that change. It had pulled him through more than once in a chance meeting with someone out of the past. Even Rickett had admitted he wouldn't have recognized him.

But now it would count for nothing. One word from Rickett, and Boa Snyder and Curt Young and all the rest would know where he was and just what he looked like. And not only them. The state police and the San Antonio Cattlemen's Association, with its connections with all the other associations throughout the West. Everywhere he went they would be waiting, knowing what he looked like, knowing who he was. It had been hard enough before. It would be impossible that way. And would the only way he could prevent it be to go along with Rickett? To drown those Pickle Bar cows?

Still filled with the bitter confusion, he hitched his mare behind the chuck wagon. He saw that the linchpin had already left. He had come up on the blind side of his own outfit, and only when he started around the other side toward the front did he see the immense, kettle-gutted man standing by a hairy black cutting horse. Marrs stopped like a snubbed bronco, sick with the shock of it. Kettle Corey turned toward him, wiping perspiration off his beefy face with a soggy, grimy bandanna. His little blue eyes were totally incongruous with the gross carnality of the rest of him. Like icy blue pools, almost hidden by the veined pouches of his eyelids, they held the chill lucidity of the patient, keen, incisive mind in that monstrous, ugly head. It was what Marrs had remembered most.

"You must be the new cook," said Kettle. "I got blotto in Dallas. Woke up in that alley behind the Oxbow about an hour ago. Slaughter will have my hide for it, I guess." He shrugged.

Marrs stared at him, the tension crawling through his belly like a snake. Was the man still playing cat-and-mouse, or did he really not recognize Marrs?

"You . . . you're with the Pickle Bar?" Marrs's voice sounded thick.

"Sure am." Kettle chuckled. "How about a cup of Triple X before I catch up with the herd?" All the time, he had been scrutinizing Marrs closely with those little eyes that saw so much. "What's your name, coosie?"

"They call me Pothooks," said Marrs.

The fat man's laughter shook his wattles. "Good name for a cook." A deep furrow dug into the flesh between his eyes, and he bent toward Marrs. "Did you ever spoil the grub for the Double Bit outfit?"

What are you doing, damn you? thought Marrs. "Never got up to the Panhandle," he said, dipping a tin cup into the one kettle of coffee he'd left on the fire. He saw that his knuckles showed white through the flesh of his hand. "Never heard of it," he said stiffly.

"I don't know," said Kettle, studying him. "You look familiar."

Handing the cup to the man, it struck Marrs for the first time that Kettle was allowing the top of his long underwear to suffice for a shirt. Out of the red wool, just above his belt, on one side, a patch about the size of a man's thumb had been torn.

Marrs's neck pulled into his shoulders slightly, and he started hitching up the horses.

"A quiet man," observed Kettle, finishing the coffee. "I like quiet men." He set the cup down, turning to hoist himself aboard his hairy animal. The rig *creaked* so loudly Marrs thought it would come apart, and Kettle almost pulled the whole saddle around beneath the horse before he finally got his weight settled. He looked down at the cook, a strange, sad expression on his sweating face. "Did it ever strike you," he said, "as short as a man's life really is, how long it can be, sometimes?" He reined his horse away to leave. "Sometimes too long."

Lips a thin bloodless line beneath his mustache, Marrs watched him trot off into the haze of cattle dust. Had the man truly not recognized him? He could conceive of no reason why Kettle should play a game. If the man were after him, he would have taken him now. Then he hadn't recognized Marrs. He was really one of the Pickle Bar hands, and had come into town like the rest of them, only going to the Oxbow out of chance. It wasn't completely impossible. Kettle hadn't known Marrs too well in those days so long ago — had only really seen him that once, at the cabin. And Marrs had been young then, a slim kid with his hair bleached so much lighter than normal by the sun and no beard yet to turn his jaw blue no matter how often he shaved. And yet the impulse to run was filling Marrs again. It had become such a natural reaction to him that it came at the slightest hint of anyone from the past. He fought it savagely, knowing that at last he had come against the walk he could run no longer. If he did, and Rickett made good his threat, it would be the beginning of the end. If Kettle hadn't recognized him, he was actually better off here. The Red River, Rickett had said. He had until then, at least. A lot of things could happen. There was Slaughter. Marrs knew his reputation. If Slaughter had refused Rickett's proposition, he wouldn't stand any pressure from Rickett. Perhaps they would clash before the Red. If Rickett crossed a man like Slaughter, anything might happen to him. It was as thin a hope as Marrs had clung to when he stayed in the Cowman's Rest on the long chance that Kettle was in Dallas by accident. And that had come through, hadn't it? Could he hope for such a break again? He could if it was all he had left. And it was.

The tension building in him made his movements stiff and jerky as he kicked out the remaining fire, closed the tailgate, which formed the chuck-box lid, and went around front to harness up the team. As he finished buckling the last trace, Guy Bedar came walking his horse up out of the bottoms. He jerked his head northward, indicating he would scout out a decent trail for the wagon to follow. The first big drops of rain started *plunking* into the canvas top of the wagon as Marrs shook the reins out. He reached for his Mackinaw and hat and hunched down to ride out the wet spell.

They rounded the herd and picked a spot in some blackjack timber for lunch. It took Marrs fifteen minutes to find dry wood, finally digging out some dead cottonwood down by a wash. He tried to set up tarps to cover the fires, but a wind had come up, and whipped the rain in under these anyway. Wet through to the skin, slopping around in the mud, fighting wind and rain, he was in an unspeakable mood when the riders started to come in. They were pushing the herd on by and arriving for lunch two and three at a time. He could not keep enough fires going to keep the coffee warm and cook the meat and bread, too. A horse got loose and kicked the lid off a Dutch oven, and, by the time Slaughter and Solo Sam came in, they had soggy, fallen bread, and cold coffee and burned steaks.

"What the hell," growled Sam. "We don't ask it to taste like cream puffs, but you could at least have it hot."

"You want it hot, you build me the fires," growled Marrs.

Slaughter swallowed his cold coffee without saying a word, but there was a faint, wise smirk on his face that Marrs had a great desire to wipe off with a dishpan. When Gail came back with the tray from their wagon, it looked as if she had been crying. She set it down, and left hurriedly, and he saw that little of the food had been eaten. It began to thunder, and all hands had to hurry back to the herd to keep it traveling quietly. It was probably the only thing that prevented a clash between Marrs and the grumbling men.

There was a green rawhide stretched beneath the chuck wagon they called the 'possum belly, and into this Marrs dumped as much of the dry cottonwood as it would carry. Then he packed up and started another wet drive. The rain had increased by now and the first big creek they reached was flooded. Dripping wet, cursing as only a disgruntled cook could curse, Marrs had to stop and cut down a couple of young trees, lashing them to either side of the wagon. Bedar was not with him now, for they needed every hand on the herd, and, alone, he started to ford the stream down a dug way hollowed out by the cattle.

When it became too deep to roll, the logs lashed on the sides of the bed floated the wagon. He made it to the far bank all right but the current swept the stern end of the wagon into the bank, smashing the off wheel. He could not repair it, and in the driving rain had to lash one of those slim logs slantwise along the bed to form a drag. This slowed him down to a snail's pace, and it was already dark by the time he reached the bed ground. The cattle were shifting mournfully in the rain, and the dull glint of a yellow slicker guided Marrs to the camp spot. A lantern burning within the covering of the linchpin gave it a sick, saffron glow in the dark. The men stood in a group beneath the blackjack timber, huddled into their slickers. There was something in their shifting, nervous silence that bothered him as he climbed off the wagon.

"What made you so damn' late?" said Pata Pala.

"It was running so easy on all four wheels I took the right rear off to make it feel more like home," said Marrs sarcastically. "I'm sure obliged to all of you for stirring me up a fire, too."

"Don't get oily," said Slaughter. "Hurry up and throw that boggy top together."

"Boggy top?" Marrs dragged some of the cottonwood from the 'possum belly, saw that it was saturated. "There ain't going to be no pie tonight. You'll be lucky if you get anything, the way this wood is."

"No boggy top," said Windy. "Why, that reminds me of the time Pecos Bill was out on roundup and the cook didn't have no pie for him. Pecos was so mad he took his rope and . . ."

"Shut up and start hunting for some dry squaw wood," growled Marrs, moving over to a bank where he began kicking the earth down in search for some buried buffalo chips.

"Sure," said the Caverango Kid, "the least we can do is help him."

"You tend to your remuda," Slaughter told him.

"But . . ."

"Kid," said Slaughter, "if you don't get out there and ride herd on that cavvy till we get supper, I'll put you to holding cows all night long without your slicker."

The boy left reluctantly, glancing in a strange way at Marrs. The cook could see them all watching him now, and sensed the rising issue. None of them made a move to aid as he finally located some dry buffalo chips and carried them over in his hat, digging out a hole beneath the bed of the wagon. He had to rip off the 'possum belly and throw the wood out to give him height enough for the fire.

Soaked to the skin, hands muddy and slippery, he was thoroughly maddened by the time he got the fire lit. He piled the cottonwood about the feeble blaze in an effort to dry it. He found that the butchered yearling had come off its ganch hooks within the wagon and the quarters and ribs were half-buried in the mud and debris he had collected fording the river. He tried to clean them off, but the muck was so impregnated in the meat he had to give this up. It was hog side, then, and the hell with them.

"Oh, no," said Waco Garrett, when he saw it. "I ate so much of that chuck wagon chicken with the last belly cheater I started grunting in my sleep and was afraid of looking around behind me for fear I'd sprouted a curly tail."

"And hot rocks, too," growled Guy Bedar when Marrs got out the biscuit makings. "That sure don't sound like boggy top to me."

Marrs wheeled from the chuck box. "Listen," he told them. "One more word and I'm going to cut loose my wolf. You're getting hog side and sinkers tonight and forgetting the rest till next sunshine. Now shut up and man at the pot." Nobody made a move. "Man at the pot," roared Marrs, "or I'll throw it in your face!"

Kettle Cory moved out of the shadows. Slaughter's face turned toward him. Those lucid blue eyes gleamed like a cat's in the dark, meeting Slaughter's gaze. Then they swung to Marrs, filled with a strange expression, and Kettle came on out and got a handful of tin cups and began to dip the coffee out of the pot beneath the chuck wagon, handing out the full cups.

They did not seem as hurried to take them as a crew that hungry should. Marrs knew what was happening, now. He wondered if it had come as a tacit agreement among them to choose this time for a test, or whether someone had instigated it. He did not believe Slaughter would approach them directly. As irritable and miserable as they were, it was a simple thing to shape their attitude with a few incidents.

Turning back to the chuck box, Marrs saw that wind had blown the canvas fly away, and the biscuits were full of water. With a bitter curse, he tossed them into a Dutch oven anyway. He had to move the coffee pot off the only fire in order to cook the bread. When the biscuits and sowbelly were done, Marrs rattled plates and forks down onto the shelf of the chuck box, stepping aside for them to get the utensils.

His glance dared anyone to say something out of line. Pata Pala was the first. After Marrs loaded his plate with sinkers and meat, the peg-legged man dipped himself out another cup of coffee. He stood back, and Marrs noticed he did not start eating until the others had been served. Then Pata Pala took a swig of the coffee, his muddy, swarthy face twisting into a grimace.

"Cold coffee, soggy bread, and hog side fit for a sheepherder," he said, and dumped it on the ground. "I ain't eating this."

"I ain't, either," added Waco Garrett, upturning his plate. "After a day like this a man deserves better. Boggy top and yearling steaks or nothing."

The others dumped their food into the mud, and Marrs stared at his bread and sowbelly slowly melting into chocolate ooze. "Pick up them plates and put 'em in the wreck pan," he said. "If that's the way you want it, you'll go without supper."

Pata Pala hooked his thumbs in the waistband of his Levi's and leaned back, spitting at his tin plate. "We ain't doing anything till you cook us some decent grub."

"You want some more grub, you cook it yourself," said Marrs.

"We dumped the other cook in the river for less than that," said Pata Pala.

"You ain't dumping this one in," Marrs told him.

"We are, if you don't throw together some more chuck."

"The hell you are," said Marrs. He saw Solo Sam moving to get around behind him, and he whirled to grab for that sawed-off machete. Pata Pala launched himself in a dive at Marrs's legs, striking him at the knees. It carried Marrs back into the mud. Marrs hooked an arm about Pata Pala's neck, holding the man onto him and slugging him in the face. Then the arm was torn aside by someone else. He saw *Don* Vargas grabbing for his other arm, and writhed aside, lashing out with a leg at the Mexican. It caught *Don* Vargas in the knee, and he bent over with a howl.

"Let him go, let him go!" shouted the Caverango Kid, running in to hook his hands in Pata Pala's broad black belt, trying to heave him off Marrs.

"Stay out of this, Kid!" shouted Waco Garrett, tearing the boy's hands free and throwing him down in the mud. Then he wheeled back and lifted a boot.

Marrs saw his intent and tried to get that free hand out of the way. But the spike heel caught it, pinning the hand down into the mud. *Don* Vargas had recovered now, and he caught the wrist while Waco held it down. Then Windy and Waco each caught a foot.

Overpowered, struggling, writhing, cursing fiendishly, Marrs was carried and dragged through the muddy grass down a dug way onto the flooded river bottoms. Here they held him while Solo Sam grabbed his hair and shoved his head underwater.

"Now," shouted Pata Pala, "are you going to cook us a decent meal?"

"The hell with you," sputtered Marrs, and jackknifed his right leg to straighten it out viciously in Windy's belly. The old man wheezed and doubled over, releasing the foot. This gave Marrs purchase against the ground, and he rolled over in their grasp, fighting like a wild animal. Sam caught his hair and shoved his head under again. Marrs was still breathing and sucked in a great lungful of water. This only made his struggles more frenzied. He felt an arm tear free and lashed out across his body at Pata Pala. He kept jackknifing the other leg, and his head jerked out of the river in time to hear Waco shouting: "He's crazy, Pata! I can't hold him . . ."

"I'll hold him," said the peg-legged man, and released his arm to hit him fully in the face. It knocked Marrs's head back into the water. Stunned for that moment, he felt them grabbing at him once more. Sam pulled his head out again.

"How about that grub?" shouted Pata Pala.

"The hell," gasped Marrs, struggling weakly.

They shoved him under again. He thought his whole being would explode with the awesome frustration of blocked breath and feeble helplessness. He seemed to float away from his own struggles for a moment, feeling them in a detached, dreamy way. Then, with a shocking jolt, he was back within their orbit, gasping, and sucking in a great breath that choked him.

"How about that grub?"

"No, damn you, no!"

Was that him? Feeble, like that? Hardly audible. In a sudden new burst of agony, his body writhed and jerked, and then it was the water again, filling his throat, his lungs, his consciousness. Hands in his hair shoving him under. Hands on his arms and legs holding their wild lashing. Hands in his hair jerking him up again.

"How about it . . . ?"

The deafening explosion blotted out Solo Sam's voice. For a moment longer, they held Marrs like that. Then he found himself released, dropped bodily into the water. Choking, gasping, he floundered to his hands and knees, crawling weakly out onto the bank. He was sick there. Finally some focus returned to his vision. He saw the men standing in a bunch where they had dropped him, staring foolishly, almost fearfully at something on the bank. His shaggy, dripping head turned that way. Gail Butler stood in the muddy dug way with a smoking, double-barreled shotgun in her hands.

"Now," she said, "if you don't leave him alone, the next thing I squeeze out of this scatter-gun will be pointed at something a lot more painful than the air."

CHAPTER
SEVEN

The rushing sound of water seemed to be the only thing in Gail Butler's consciousness. The stupor of sleep lay across her in heavy, oppressive layers. She seemed to grope through them one by one, until full awareness of where she was came to her. Marrs was in her mind, somehow. What was that water? The Red River already? How many days from Dallas, now? She had lost count. And how many days since the men had hoorawed Marrs down in that creek? Three, or four? Time seemed to have lost significance, seemed to have become one blur of morning steaming up out of the earth and noon baking the land so dry it cracked beneath the feet and night bringing spring rains that turned the ground to a morass. And yet through all that blur, she could still see Marrs clearly, like a savage, shaggy animal, writhing in their midst down in that creek. Why was he in her mind so much? Was it the mystery of his past? Or something else? Had that been last night?

She heard Paul draw in a heavy breath beside her, and looked toward him reluctantly. He must have just awakened, and felt her eyes on him.

"Gail," he murmured, "get me some paregoric."

She felt of his head. "Paul, you haven't got any fever."

"I feel bad," he said. "Get me some, I said."

"Paul, I'm afraid to have you use too much. If you keep it up like this, there won't be any left for Waco."

"The hell with Waco," he said, thrashing about in his blankets. "Get me some paregoric, Gail, or do I have to go out and get it myself? I never saw such a woman. Don't give a damn about her own husband. So it's Waco now."

"What's Waco . . . what do you mean? I just . . ."

"You just got tired of Slaughter, so now you're playing around with Waco Garrett. Maybe it brings out the maternal instinct in you . . . a man with his insides so banged up he can't think straight. Pathetic, isn't it? Much more pathetic than your own husband . . ."

"Oh, Paul, stop it, for God's sake."

She wheeled and fumbled into her robe, crawling from the wagon blindly, unable to see through the tears. She stood against the tailgate, breathing heavily. How could two people start out with so much beauty and end up with so much bitterness?

She remembered the laughter, the kisses, the dancing. How handsome he had been then, how charming. Could a man actually change that radically? Once more she found herself going back over the pattern of it. When Paul had inherited the Pickle Bar, it had been the biggest outfit south of San Antonio. Then, four years after their marriage, came that awful winter of 1871. It had ruined a lot of spreads. It didn't leave much of the Pickle Bar.

Paul had broken his leg that year, just about the time the full weight of the terrible winter was being felt. It had taken so long to heal. If he had been on his feet, he could have saved the outfit. How many times had he told her that? Told everybody that? It seemed to have become the greeting of the house that year. Those had been the first blows, and, after that, the pattern formed itself clearly. Each succeeding blow seemed to have wiped off a little of the veneer. She hadn't wanted to believe it in him, at first. Had refused to face it. The romance of it was too precious to a girl on this barren frontier. But now all the romance was gone, leaving something sordid, ugly. She found it difficult even to retain bitterness, now. It was only dull, aching, with her constantly. She had taken over, had managed to salvage something, riding like a man through that blizzard when word came of the die-up along the northern drift fence, hiring border hoppers from the brush, over Paul's protests, to give her a big enough crew to hold the animals from drifting so far away they could not be tended.

He had fought her the next year, too, when she wanted to send every steer they had north, to take advantage of the high beef prices. But she had gone ahead, selling high at Ellsworth and buying cheap the next year at Matagorda to restock their pastures. And the year after, Paul had ridden north with the trail herd himself. She still wasn't clear in her mind about the wound. She didn't know yet whether it had happened before or during the jayhawkers' attack. It seemed a slight wound, at that, when she heard about it from the crew, upon their return. But there was something about infection setting in, and making Paul delirious during the attack. A man couldn't really be blamed for losing his herd if he was lying in his blankets delirious when it was attacked.

She found herself headed toward the chuck wagon, with the *rattling* of pans coming dimly from its rear end. The rain had stopped, but the sun had not yet risen. A thick, sticky ground fog sucked at the wheel hubs. And under all the other sounds was the rush of the Red River. She found Marrs building his fires from more of those buried buffalo chips, and asked him for the medicine. He turned without meeting her eyes, moving with those short, stabbing steps to the wagon.

"Did it humiliate you that badly to have a woman stop them at the creek?" she said, taking the bottle from his hand.

He met her eyes for the first time. That sullen reserve started to narrow the heavy, sensuous lids.

"Don't be childish," she said. "If a man had stopped them, you wouldn't take this attitude with him. What's the difference? You shouldn't feel humiliated. It's happened to other cooks. You can't fight the whole crew."

He scuffed his boot across the ground, staring down at it, then emitted a short, harsh laugh, shrugging. "I guess you're right. I didn't thank you yet, Missus Butler."

"Forget it," she said. Then she frowned, shaking the bottle. "There isn't much paregoric left, is there?"

"I guess not," he told her.

82

She handed it back to Marrs. "You keep it for Waco. It's the only thing that will help his old injuries, and we don't run into a town where we can get another bottle till Kansas."

"Won't it cause a row?" he asked.

She stared at him, unable, for a moment, to fathom his meaning.

"Your husband," he said.

She drew a quick little breath.

He made an apologetic motion with one hand. "I don't mean to get personal, but being this near the linchpin, I can't help hearing some of it." He paused, studying something, a faint, humorless smile catching at one corner of his mouth. "You know, it's funny how a man can get to know someone without ever seeing him. I've heard the crew talk about Paul Butler. I've never seen you come out of that linchpin smiling. I've heard him yell things at you I wouldn't say to my dog. You deserve something better than that, Missus Butler."

She bowed her head, shaking it. "Let's not talk about it, Pothooks."

"Why not?" he said. "Are you afraid to admit it, even to yourself? Is he really that sick?"

"I don't know," she said, glancing helplessly from side to side. "He has fever, sometimes. He did catch that cold before we hit Dallas. He bathed in the creek and stood too long in the wind or something."

"Just about the time you began having trouble with the cook, maybe?"

She looked up, eyes wide in protest. But his eyes were not mocking. They were filled with those kindling little lights she had seen back in the Cowman's Rest, seeming to give his face a smile, although he wasn't actually smiling. It took all the defiance from her. She lowered her eyes again, drawing a deep breath.

"I guess so."

"And what was the trouble before that?"

"I don't know. A lot of it . . ."

"And him always seeming to be sick. I guess some people are like that. They can't face failure. I had an aunt once. She spent most of her time in bed. Funny part of it was, I don't think she was actually sick."

"But he is." She raised her head again, speaking almost pleadingly. "He is sick, Pothooks."

"Sure. A person can talk himself into anything. Probably even without knowing it. But I never saw it in a man before."

"Oh, stop it," she said, wheeling away. "Stop it!"

He caught her arm to keep her from going. His voice was surprisingly soft. "I'm sorry. I didn't mean to hurt you. I thought maybe you needed somebody to talk with. You can't keep it inside all the time."

She pulled away. "And maybe we'll put the linchpin a little farther away next time we stop," she said coldly. She saw the surprised, hurt look across his face, and then the withdrawal, as palpable as if he had backed away, retiring into that surly, brooding shell, lowering his head till she could not see his eyes, and turning away from her. She reached out to grasp his arm. "Pothooks, I'm sorry . . ."

"Forget it," he said. "I got breakfast to make."

She turned again, close to tears, and walked blindly back toward the linchpin. Why had she let him probe so deeply? He had voiced doubts and questions that she had deliberately kept herself from facing. Had she wanted to cling to romance that desperately? It was a precious thing to a girl in such a vast and lonely land.

She shook her head bitterly. It was more than romance, she told herself. It was the loyalty of a wife to her husband. Maybe Paul's tantrums depressed her and wore her down. But basically she couldn't do him such an injustice. No person was his normal self when he was sick. Give him a chance. A good year with the cattle, time to regain his health, and he would be the handsome, dashing man she had known before; they would know again the fulfillment and gaiety of the life they had known those first years. Any man could be bowed by trouble. She had to give him a chance.

She started to climb into the linchpin. Then, unable to face the tantrum she knew would come when she told Paul there was no paregoric to be had, she stepped back down and walked around the wagon, moving aimlessly toward the fringe of trees. She rounded an island of soggy oak, and brought up in a startled way. But it was only Windy, digging up more buffalo chips to put in a rawhide bucket.

"Did Marrs ask you to do this?" She frowned.

Windy cackled. "Ast me? He ordered me, with that machete meat cleaver over my head. That dunking the other night didn't take any of his vinegar out."

85

She studied him a long, silent period, and finally asked what had been on her mind from the beginning. "Windy, who was Lee Marrs Benton?"

The hoarfrost of the old man's eyebrows lifted sharply. He straightened slowly, putting a hand against his back. The expression filling his eyes was almost frightening.

"You know," she said.

"Think I didn't figger it out, the minute he dabbed that hooley-ann to the Kid's horse," said Windy. "Not many people knew what that M stood for. But when a man stands as high in his profession as Lee M. Benton did, his skill marks him better'n any name ever would."

"What's the story, Windy?" she said.

He went back to picking at the chips, unwilling to look at her as he spoke. "You remember how mavericking was regarded right after the War Between the States. Texas men had been away from their cattle a long time. Five years of increase was running around, unbranded. It's easy enough to tell what brand a suckling calf should bear by the mamma it's tailing, but when you get a five-year-old bull that's been popping the brush so long his horns are mossy, it's almost impossible to tell who he belongs to. There were so many of these mavericks that it became the custom, for a time, to throw your own brand on anything that had no obvious connection with a known outfit. A lot of big cattlemen got their start that way. I worked with Boa Snyder when he started his first outfit purely on the mavericks he'd branded."

"That was just about the time I came from Missouri to marry Paul," said Gail. "I remember. Texas was cattle rich. The big outfits had more cows than they could herd, and no markets for them. They probably encouraged men like Boa Snyder to maverick."

"At first they did," said Windy. "But when the northern markets opened up, and a cow became worth fifteen, twenty dollars, mavericking was outlawed. A lot of men like Boa Snyder pulled out just in time to save themselves getting the stamp of rustler. In fact there's some suspicion that Snyder and Curt Young and a few others kept on mavericking undercover a long time after it was outlawed. You probably arrived just after the Benton case. A regular war was declared on rustlers and maverickers. A brand inspector for the San Antonio Cattlemen's Association was down in Nueces County on a hot trail that he claimed was going to blow the lid off the whole thing. He was found near Corpus Christi. He'd been tied to a mesquite tree and tortured to death. Spanish dagger thorns were in his eyes, and his feet was near roasted off in sotol stalks."

Gail could not help the horrified sound she made, and Windy looked up, nodding. "That's the way most folks felt. It sent a reg'lar army of Association men and local officers into the brush to clean out them maverickers once and for all. Lee Benton was known to be a leader of one group. He was just a kid . . . seventeen, eighteen . . . but he'd been an orphan and growed up pretty fast, and he'd already made something of a reputation, mavericking with Boa Snyder and Curt Young and the others. But he didn't have sense to quit before it became outlawed. One of the Association men was Gary Carson, an old saddlemate of Benton's, known and loved by everybody along the border. He and three detectives surrounded Benton in a shack south of Corpus Christi. The others wanted to fill the shack with lead, but Carson argued them into talking it over with Benton. He went out holding a white handkerchief on a stick, told Benton the situation, that he was surrounded with no hope of escaping, and that he'd save his life by coming out. Benton refused, and, when Carson turned around, Benton shot him in the back."

She felt sick, deep down, and stared in horror at Windy. "Why haven't you told me this before?"

"I figured you knew," he said. He went on kicking aimlessly at the buffalo chips. "It was the most useless, wanton killing I ever heard of, I guess, and the brutality of it immediately hooked Benton up with that brand inspector who'd been tortured. The detectives filled the shack with lead, thought they'd killed Benton. But he lived to see trial. Feelings were so high that people forgot about the other maverickers down there. For six months, the only talk below the Nueces was Lee M. Benton. They tried to lynch him a couple of times. The mystery of the whole thing is why Benton didn't get executed. The first judge passed that sentence on him. Then there came along a decision from the State Supreme Court commuting it to life imprisonment. A couple of years later, he escaped and disappeared. I don't know if he ever really left the cattle country. If he did, he come back again. I can understand that. I don't think I could stand to stay away long. I think I'd come back, too, even if it meant taking a chance on getting killed. It gets you, that way."

"Do the other men here know?"

He shrugged. "Some might have guessed. Kettle Corey is the only one who knew Benton personally. He was one of the detectives who trapped Benton in that shack. If he's recognized Pothooks as Lee Marrs Benton, he hasn't given any sign. I don't know what he's doing."

"But you didn't speak," she said. "That's what I can't understand. Suspecting Pothooks Marrs of being that man . . ."

"I thought of quitting. Oncet I felt sick, thinking of whose food I was eating." He lifted his head, staring at her. "But there's sort of a code among 'punchers, Missus Butler. It leaves a man's past be. There's a lot of men in Texas with ugly things behind them. I made a dry camp with King Fisher oncet, and didn't ast him why he'd murdered ten men, not counting Mexicans. If I had, it would probably have been seventeen."

"That's why you're tolerating this man," she said scornfully. "Not for any code. You're afraid of him, you're afraid to speak out against him!"

An indefinable, hurt expression lined Windy's face, and he lowered his head, nodding. "Maybe you're right. A lot of salt has spilled out of a man when he reaches my age."

"I won't have a man like that working for the Pickle Bar!" said Gail. She whirled and started back to the wagons, aware for the first time that the men were saddling up, the plates still piled untouched on the chuck-box lid. *Don* Vargas was trying to cinch up his prancing, pirouetting black horse.

"Hold still there, you *chingado*, you *rumbero*, you *porfido* . . . "

"If you'd stop using that baby talk on him and try some real cuss words, he might mind," said Pata Pala disgustedly, swinging onto his hairy cutting horse and jamming that peg leg through the shortened stirrup.

"Baby talk!" exploded *Don* Vargas. "You don't know what profanity is till you've heard a real Mexican *vaquero* swear. *¡Sinvergüenza!* What can match that in English?"

"It don't curl my ears," said Pata Pala.

Gail ran up to them, asking what had happened, and the peg-legged man nodded toward Slaughter, already out getting the herd off the bed ground. "Bob says the river's getting higher every minute, and wants to put the cattle over before it gets too rough. Didn't even let us wait for breakfast."

Hurriedly she turned back toward the wagons. Marrs was forgotten in the excitement. He had already kicked out the fires and hitched up his team, and she watched him drive toward the bank with a mingled intensity of emotions. Finally she turned to hitch up her own horses and mount the linchpin's seat. Paul crawled out, a blanket over his shoulders.

"What's going on?" he said bitterly. "Where's that paregoric?"

90

"We'll have to get it later, Paul," she evaded. "Why don't you stay out and watch them put the cattle across? It always thrills me so."

"Oh, hell," he said, spitting aside. But he sat down on the seat, staring woodenly ahead, a resentment twitching his face at each jolt of the wagon.

The river swept full to the banks before them, chuckling and gurgling at the mouths of the dug ways. The great chocolate expanses of muddy water ripped asunder suddenly by a smashed tree vomited from beneath, to ride one hundred feet on a streak of foaming white water, before it was sucked down again in a whirlpool formed by a hole dug in the bottom by the rampage. The cattle approached the dug way reluctantly, bawling and lowing.

A steer the color of a sandhill crane balked at the mouth of the dug way. Behind him a beef of blended gold and brown and black, which the Mexicans called *hosco golondrino*, dug its sharp hoofs into the mud and refused to push the steer. They piled up like a backwash behind it, brindles and blues — mulberry blues and ring-streaked blues and speckled blues — browns with bay points and bays with brown points. Their great long horns *crashed* and *rang* against one another with the sound of a thousand fencers. The raucous bedlam of their bawling rose above the roar of the turbulent river.

Then it was the swing men, pushing in from either side to force that Grullo steer out into the water and make the *hosco golondrino* follow awkwardly, long bony legs sprawling out like a fallen child, thrusting its heavy, ludicrous head forward with eyes rolling white.

Slaughter was right in the middle. No denying that. The first man in the water, swimming his big roping mare right alongside the *hosco golondrino*, leading them on with his voice as much as his actions. It was a scene that could not help but thrill Gail. She was lost in thought.

> *Oh, I'll shake this job tomorrow,*
> *Pack my sougans on a hoss,*
> *And pull my freight for Texas,*
> *Where there ain't no dad-blamed boss . . . .*

It was Solo Sam on the swing, his lean figure swaying in the saddle as he came in from the side to force the bulk of the herd into the dug way and out into the water. After him, from the other flank, came Guy Bedar. After another space of plunging bawling animals filling the dug way, Kettle Cory's great head appeared above the cattle. His shaggy chopping horse stepped down through that slippery mud so daintily it was hard to believe he was packing close to three hundred pounds on his back. But a heavy man could ride as light as a little one if he was good, and Gail had never seen an abused horse in Kettle's string.

Then came *Don* Vargas on the prancing, nervous black. The cattle were spreading out in deeper water now, pushed by the oncoming ranks behind. Slaughter was near the middle, and Gail could barely hear his voice, calling orders to the men. Once, Gail thought, she saw Guy Bedar's narrow head turn back toward the chuck wagon, where it had halted on the bank a few yards below the linchpin. It directed her gaze that way.

Marrs was busy lashing logs onto the sides of his wagon, oblivious to the scene. Beside Gail, Paul shifted morosely in his blanket, huddled over on the seat, watching the stirring pageant indifferently.

"Slaughter had better send enough men back to get this wagon over safely," he muttered petulantly.

Gail sighed. "I'm sure he will, Paul."

"Hey, Bedar!" bawled Windy from the bank. "You're pushing that *golondrino* away from its trail mate! Get them separated and you'll have a mill, sure!"

There was a sharp note to his cry that stiffened Gail on the seat. She had traveled north with enough herds to know the habit of steers choosing a trail mate and traveling a thousand miles without leaving its side. More than once, she had seen a steer bunch-quit to hunt for its mate, refusing to return to the herd until they had found each other again. Evidently the *golondrino* steer had been traveling with the slate-colored leader. She recognized the tone of its call now, the toss of its head. Somehow, Bedar had shoved a cut of steers between this one and the leader, and the *golondrino* had halted completely, swirled around and around by the tide, bawling helplessly for its mate. The Grullo leader looked around and, seeing its mate gone, turned to swim back to the *golondrino*.

"Stop that leader!" howled Slaughter. "He'll turn the whole herd in a circle!"

Bedar left the *golondrino* to swim his horse through the outer fringe toward the leader, and Kettle came in, the other way. It looked as if Kettle would reach its flank and turn the beast, but some clumsy maneuver of Bedar's turned another cut of steers between Kettle and the slate-colored one.

"Get out of there, damn you!" bellowed Slaughter.

"What the hell!" shouted Bedar. "I can't help what those critters get in their mind!"

He wheeled his horse to swim it out of the growing jam, barely escaping the circular motion of animals that the turning back of the leader had started. The positions of the two steers were reversed now. The whole bunch was beginning to turn like a great wheel, with the leader actually fighting in toward the center, thinking its mate was still there. Actually the *golondrino* had been swept to the outer fringes by the circling pressure. The bawling of the steers had become so loud and excited by this time that the shouts of the men farther out were no longer audible.

More and more animals were pouring down out of the dug way, into the river, excited by the noise and violence, and Windy and the other men on the bank could not hold them. The circling mass of steers in the water was growing larger and larger, packed in tighter and tighter.

Evidently thinking that, if he could get the *golondrino* separated from the rest, the leader would see its mate and break for it and stop the mill, Slaughter had waited till the spinning fringe carried the *golondrino* around past him, and had roped the animal's horns. But the *golondrino* started battling. Dirty yellow water spouted up about them, hiding man

94

and beast for an instant. Slaughter's head appeared out of the whirl, then the animal's horns. It was pulling him on back into the other steers. Gail found herself standing on the seat, screaming at Slaughter.

"Don't fight them that way, Bob, you'll only spook the whole bunch . . ."

But Slaughter was in his towering rage. She could feel its awesome force at this distance. She could see how viciously he was spurring his horse, so losing his head that he was pitting his own weight and strength against the bull's struggles, his whole massive body jerking backward in the saddle every time he pulled on that rope. Vainly Kettle and Solo Sam were trying to wedge their animals in on the flanks to turn the mill, but their efforts were lost in the general wheeling motion of the whole herd. It was rapidly becoming a great vortex of frenzied steers, that Grullo the hub of the wheel. Even Paul could see how it was going now. He was leaning forward on the seat beside Gail.

"He'll lose them," he said between his teeth. "He'll lose the whole bunch. Damn you, Slaughter, they'll drown each other and they'll all go down!"

It was ghastly to watch, that great, turgid, circular motion of bawling, crazed animals, becoming faster and faster. Countless horns flashed and dipped and disappeared in the rocking, rolling bodies. The first dead steer floated into sight fifty yards away from the herd. He had been crushed and trampled under, the carcass kicked and whirled along beneath those hoofs until it was free of the herd, then thrown up from the violent tide of the river like so much driftwood, to whirl and spin on down the turbulent tide until it disappeared. The mill was in full tilt now. Kettle and Waco spun around on the fringe helplessly, Slaughter out there still battling madly with the leader, his terrible rage blinding him to what was happening. The awesome, certain finality of it brought the name unconsciously to Gail's lips.

"Pothooks," she said. "Pothooks."

It was as if he had heard, although she had not spoken it loud enough to reach him. There was a violent blur of movement past her, and she saw him running. The Caverango Kid had left his remuda in timber, and brought his horse up on a higher portion of the bank above the wagons to watch the mill, and it was toward him Pothooks ran.

"Give me those gut hooks, Kid!" shouted the cook, grabbing for the Kid's right boot and unbuckling the spur. He leaned down to snap it on his own boot, and by that time the Kid had lifted his other foot up to take off the right spur. Pothooks grabbed this and put it on, and then pulled the Kid down off his horse.

The cook spun the animal around to get on the left side, jumping high so that his left foot hit the oxbow the same time his rump hit the saddle. Then he raked the spurs across the animal's flanks and drove it off the bank in a great leap. Man and beast disappeared completely in the water, to bob up ten yards beyond, swirled around and around by the heavy, churning tide. Then the undertow formed by the milling herd caught him, pulling the horse in fast against the outer fringe of cattle.

"He can't do anything!" said Paul shrilly. "Nobody could break that mill from the outside now. They're lost, Gail, they're through . . ."

But Marrs was not trying to stop them from the outside. He had jumped from his horse onto the backs of the cattle. They were packed in so close it was like walking across logs. A tossing horn caught him across the belly, knocking him backward, and for a moment Gail thought he was gone. He slipped between two great heaving bodies up to the waist. But before they could pin him, he had caught another horn, pulling himself up. Then, dodging those great slashing horns, ducking aside from a violent, blind toss of a brindle head, jumping the heaving hump of a speckled white steer, he made his way toward the center of the mill. She could see him swing an arm in Slaughter's direction to emphasize the words his roaring, surly shout carried to Gail.

"Quit fighting that *golondrino*, damn you! He's just exciting hell out of all the rest!"

Slaughter at last must have realized what his actions were causing, for he tried to get slack enough in his rope to slip it off the steer he had been battling. But the steer kept shifting away, tangling the rope up among the other cattle. The rope was tied hard and fast on the saddle horn of Slaughter's rig. Seeing that he could not free it from the animal, he began to tear wildly at the knot on his horn. But it had become wet, and Gail could see he was not having any success. The *golondrino* was going its merry, wild way, pulling Slaughter with it. Its crazy bawls and frenzied struggles exhorting the rest of the herd into a rising, maddened crescendo of sound and movement.

Gail saw Marrs's mouth move in a curse that did not carry this far, and he whipped his Walker from his belt. Its sullen *boom* beat flatly across the other bedlam. Once. Twice. The *golondrino* heaved half its bulk out of the water, blood spurting from the wounds to redden the tide about it.

"Now cut it loose, damn you!" he screamed at Slaughter. The trail boss fished his Barlow from a hip pocket, whipping it open, and slashed at the rope in a desperate effort to cut it before the drowning steer pulled his horse under. Balancing delicately on the constantly shifting animals, kicking and jumping and rolling like a logger in white water, leaping from back to back, falling to his knees and scrambling erect again, face bloody from the slash of a horn, shirt ripped across his belly, Marrs finally made it to the Grullo leader. He straddled the beast like a horse, grasping its horns to hang on. Then Gail understood why he had gotten those spurs.

His legs were out of sight, but his torso jerked with the force of raking the beast with those gut hooks, and the burning pain caused the Grullo to rear up, emitting its agony in a great bawling bellow. It had been resigning itself apathetically to the general movement of the herd, allowing itself to be spun around and around by the others, but this violent surging motion carried it against them in a decisive movement. Marrs pointed its head with his grip on those horns, spurring it once more.

Again the steer gave a great, leaping surge. It broke the inner ranks this time, turning the others partway in the same direction. Once more, Marrs spurred the animal. Its bawling sound held the frenzy of unbearable pain. Madly it fought forward to escape those terrible gut hooks, trampling under a great brindle heifer, literally crawling across the back of a floundering black. Others turned to get out of the way, and centrifugal pressure forced still others into the path the Grullo had left behind, turning after it. This formed a gradually growing movement in one direction.

The pressure of this began to turn the outer ranks, and gave Waco and Solo Sam and Kettle a chance to get free and help keep the movement going. And all the time, Marrs was driving the lead steer out.

Scrambling, bawling, fighting, screaming, the beast finally broke the back of the milling ranks, and they began to give more easily. Finally Marrs was on the fringe, and in another moment would be free.

Gail saw it happen the same time she heard the cry. It was a sharp, frightened cry, hardly loud enough to be noticed above the other sounds, but it turned her head enough to see Solo Sam go off his horse. He had been working in the fringes, but there was still enough of the mill left to trap him in a swirl of earthen-colored bodies and flailing, clashing horns.

"It's Sam!" cried Waco from near the shore. "I can't reach him, Slaughter! You're the nearest! Get him before he goes under!"

Slaughter had cut himself free of the *golondrino* and, with his rope trailing in the water, had moved his swimming horse over near enough to Marrs to take advantage of the breaking mill, wedging himself into a rank of cows and turning them toward the opposite bank.

"He'll be all right!" he shouted. "Tell him to tail his horse! I leave these critters now and we'll lose them again!"

"He ain't got no horse, damn you!" shouted Waco, trying to drive his own animal through a solid phalanx of cattle in a futile attempt to reach Sam. "Oh, damn you, Slaughter, you could do it, you're the only one!"

Either Slaughter had not heard him, or ignored him, for he was driving his ranks of cattle into a straight run for the bank, breaking the mill for good with the pressure of Marrs's Grullo coming in behind. Marrs turned to look back, and then scrambled erect on the Grullo, and began to make his way back across them that way. The wagon seat trembled with Paul's violent movement beside Gail. His voice beat vitriolically against her ears: "Oh, no, you damn' fool, they'll mill again . . . they'll mill again!"

She felt the appalled darkness filling the glance she turned on her husband. He saw it, and a surprised look crossed his face. Her mouth twisted down with more expression than she had allowed him to see in months, and then she turned back. With the drive of the Grullo gone, the cattle had started to turn back into the mill, packing together again, and it was across this that Marrs went, sometimes on his belly, moving inevitably back toward the spot Solo Sam had gone under. Gail's breath blocked her throat with the certainty that he would never make it.

But he did. And when he reached the two steers swimming at the spot where Sam had gone down, he jammed down a leg, separating their dripping, shiny bodies. A bloody arm popped up, and he swung a hand for it, missing. The arm disappeared. Face turned down, Marrs crawled across the back of a huge mulberry stag, moving inward on the mill. Then he reached down between the mulberry and the next steer, grasping for something Gail couldn't see.

There was a violent shift in the ranks, and he disappeared between the two bodies. Gail heard the strangled sound she made, and found herself standing on the wagon seat, staring fixedly out there.

Marrs's head bobbed up again. A thick, hairy arm hooked over the back of a black steer, the shirt sleeve torn off to the shoulder. Muscles rippled like fat snakes beneath the white skin, pulling him belly down over the black. He had a body slung under his other arm. It was Solo Sam, a slack, limp figure in the cook's grip.

Marrs got to his hands and knees on their backs once more. This last trip was the most harrowing thing Gail had ever experienced. It had been deadly enough making his way across that precarious corduroy surface of constantly shifting, heaving, turning backs alone. Now he had to carry Sam with him. Twice Marrs slipped and almost went under. Waco Garrett was near enough to shore so that Gail could see tears streaming down his face every time its profile turned far enough this way. The Caverango Kid had waded out to his waist in the river, staring in a charmed way at the scene. It was about as far to shore as it was back to the Grullo, and Marrs had chosen the steer.

Doggedly, stubbornly, tenaciously Marrs crawled and bellied and snaked across the steers, jammed up again like logs. He was apparently too played out even to try to gain his feet. His shirt was ripped from him and his whole body was bloody. Once, a shift in their movement flashed his face this way. It was twisted in a ghastly, fixed grimace that showed the bone whiteness of teeth beneath the black line of his mustache.

Finally he made it, throwing Sam belly down across the Grullo, straddling it once more as a man would sit a horse. And once more began that game of breaking the mill. The jerk of his body told of the vicious swipe of those spurs, the screaming lunge of the tiring steer, the ranks giving with painful, maddening reluctance.

When he finally broke free, with the mill stopped, and the other steers following their slate leader to shore, pushed on by the riders, Gail found herself still standing in the seat, her whole body so stiff the muscles were twitching with tension across her back and belly and legs. With a sob, she collapsed onto the seat. The Caverango Kid was still standing up to the waist in the turgid, murky flow, hands fisted at his sides, staring across at Marrs.

"My God," he was saying, over and over. "My God. My God . . ."

Gail saw the Grullo reach the other side. Marrs slid off and lay on his belly in the shallows. Kettle sidled in and dragged him to dry ground, dropping him once more to lie movelessly on his stomach. They dragged Solo Sam off, sitting him up against a tree. Windy and Pata Pala came by with the drags of the herd, putting it into the muddy water. Gail found herself huddled over on the seat, crying very quietly.

CHAPTER
EIGHT

There was something reassuring about the soft *crackle* of campfires, after the terrible, violent uncertainty of a few hours before. The rich, humid scent of wet spring earth filled the night. Bob Slaughter leaned against the head of the chuck wagon, hands in the hip pockets of his Levi's. He could not help marvel at the incredible vitality of Marrs. The man had recovered from that grueling experience in half an hour, and had been able to help the men get the wagons across the Red, after the herd had been safely put onto ground. Now, five miles north of the Red, he was going about his duties of the evening meal as casually as if it were the end of an ordinary day.

Slaughter shrugged. That was youth. Maybe Marrs was younger than he looked. Then a bitter, driving reaction to that swept up in Slaughter. Youth, hell. What did that have to do with it? He could match Marrs every foot of the way. He could take on any kid half his age and play him out and still have enough vinegar left to dance all night. Youth didn't have anything to do with it. He thrust his body away from the wagon, walking over toward Waco Garrett, where the man sat, cross-legged, toying with his food. He felt Windy's eyes on him, and cut a glance at him. Windy was looking his way, but a blank, opaque withdrawal filled the old man's eyes as he met Slaughter's glance. Slaughter turned back to Waco as he halted by him.

"You feel good enough to ride first guard with Pata Pala tonight?"

Waco looked up. There was a moment of empty silence. Part of it was filled with Waco's palpable effort to relax the drawn muscles of his face. "Sure, Bob. I'm all right."

"What's the matter?" asked Slaughter.

Waco's eyes seemed to be looking right through him. "Nothing, Bob. My stomach's all right."

"I don't mean that," said Slaughter. "What's the matter?"

"Nothing, Bob," said Waco in a hollow voice. He rose and took his dish over to the wreck pan, dumping it in. At the off wheel of the wagon, he let his eyes pass across Slaughter once more. Then he was beyond, going for his night horse in the remuda.

"Don't you really know what the matter is, Bob?" asked Gail, from over to one side. He wheeled to see her standing in some scrub elm, the buffalo brush forming a silver background for the soft folds of her calico skirt. Her face was pale. Her eyes caught the light like a cat's, gleaming, flat and green, for an instant, then lost in shadow with the slight turn of her head. He moved over to her, running a hand irritably through the yellow mane of his hair. They were out of earshot from the others here, and he spoke in a guttural, frustrated voice.

"What do you mean, Gail?"

"I'm talking about Solo Sam," she said.

"What about Solo Sam," he said.

"Don't spar, Bob," she told him.

"Listen," he said. "The boy took his chances just like the rest of us. If I'd left those leaders, the mill would have started all over again and we'd have lost the whole herd."

"Is that worth a boy's life?" she said.

"Is that the thanks I get for saving your herd?"

"You," she said, letting something caustic thread it.

"Oh, hell," he said. "You know what I mean. Of course it was Marrs. It was just the choice I made, that's all. I was thinking of your herd, Gail. Of you. If our places had been switched, I wouldn't have expected Sam to come after me."

"And if you had the choice to make over again, it would be the same one." It was more a statement than a question.

He stared at her, knowing the incrimination his answer would cause him. "It would," he said quietly.

"At least you have the courage of your convictions," she said, and again she allowed some of her feelings to color the words, and it was more loathing this time.

"Don't say it like that, Gail," he told her. "A man has his decisions to make and he makes them according to his ethics."

"And they show what kind of a man he is more than all the talk in the world," she said.

"Did I ever try to deny what I was?"

"Honesty isn't the only virtue," she told him.

106

He grasped her arms, moving in closer to her, excited by the faint warmth exuding from her body, the scented nearness of her, the pale halo of taffy hair just beneath his chin.

"Don't be like that, Gail. I don't care if the men hold it against me. A trail boss gets the blame for it all, anyway. Nothing he does is right. I'd expect it from them. But you . . ."

"What about me?"

"Gail," he muttered. "Would it help if I admitted it was a mistake?"

"No," she said. "Because I'd know you were lying. At least be consistent, Bob. It's one of the few things left in you I can admire."

She tore loose and moved toward the linchpin. She passed Marrs about twenty feet away, but there was something in the fleeting, almost furtive glance she put across him that raised a strange, indefinable jealousy in Slaughter. He made a guttural sound deep in his throat. Then, releasing the anger in movement, he headed toward the remuda in a long, driving stride, like the pace of a huge, caged beast, calling to the Caverango Kid to cut out his roping horse. It was his favorite animal, a big Quarter horse, with a black stripe down his back. He took it from the boy and led it over to his gear, thrown down a little apart from the other sougans. He heaved his heavy Porter rig up with one arm, and, as he was taking a hitch in the trunk strap of the latigo, *Don* Vargas wandered over.

"You going for a drink at the Station House, maybe."

"Maybe," said Slaughter angrily.

"Can I go, too, maybe?"

Slaughter turned to face him squarely, jaw muscles bulging in the ruddy, weathered flesh. "What do you think about Sam?"

Don Vargas shrugged narrow shoulders. "I always say a man takes his own chances on the trail, Roberto."

"At least I've got one intelligent man in my crew," said Slaughter, tugging the trunk strap cinch home with a vicious grunt. "Come on. Let's go."

Grinning, *Don* Vargas ran out to get his horse. He came back with the prancing black, its coat glistening from the recent rain. Slaughter glanced disgustedly at it.

"Why don't you trade that weedy Arab for a decent cow pony? He couldn't cut a biscuit."

"*¡Valgame Dios!*" swore the Mexican, heaving his center-fire rig on. "You are talking about a descendant in a straight line from El Morzillo, the war horse Cortez himself brought to Mexico in his conquest, one of the first horses on this continent. He is no weedy Arab, *amigo*. He is a barb of the hottest blood, and he'll make your Texas cow ponies look like prairie dogs."

"Then beat me to the Station House!" shouted Slaughter, raking his roper with his Peteneckey's.

"*¡Hola!*" shouted *Don* Vargas, and his immense cartwheel spurs made a flash in the firelight, and his black mount leaped forward.

They raced right through the middle of camp and Windy had to move fast to get out of their way, spilling his supper on the ground. Slaughter didn't give a damn, letting the wind whip his hat brim back against its crown, trying to empty out all the gathered venom of the past hours in the wild ride.

They trampled through scarlet mallow and dodged into a motte of blackjack. Slaughter ducked a branch and it knocked his hat off to swing behind him in the wind by the tie thong around his neck. He bent low over the horse, glorying in its delicate response to the slightest pressure of his reins, veering it around a big cottonwood with the slightest switch of his hand, turning it out of the trees into a muddy, rutted road by barely touching the off rein against its neck.

The Quarter blood in the roper had given it the jump on *Don* Vargas, but now the barb's bottom was beginning to tell, and Slaughter could hear the sloppy beat of hoofs in the muck behind. He gave the roper those Peteneckey's again, and it surged into a greater burst of speed, barrel heaving in a labored way between his legs. He saw a big Murphy freighter stalled hub deep in the mud ahead and tore about one side of it, leaving the angry shouts of the splattered teamsters behind. Again he drove the spurs into the roper, and headed it into a crazy, headlong run for the last quarter mile to the deadfall at Red River Station.

He pulled his heaving, steaming horse back on its hocks before the low-roofed log building set on the bluff and jumped off, throwing the reins across the hitch rack with half a dozen others. He shouldered through the door without waiting for *Don* Vargas. It was an evil den, with sawdust covering the floor and reeking of stale cigars and rotten liquor and foul river mud. There were already a dozen trail drivers and hands at the round deal tables, and they hailed him.

He went over to where a bald, scarred man with a broken nose and mashed ears stood behind the bar, serving the liquor in big tin mugs from a row of barrels set on racks against the wall.

"None of that tanglefoot, Katz," he said, leaning his elbows on the bar. "Give me some decent sugar top."

"For you, Bob, anything," said Katz, leaning beneath the bar to open a bung there.

The ride had blotted out Slaughter's snaky mood for a moment, but he could feel it coming back now. *Don* Vargas came through the door, wiping his sweating face with a red bandanna.

"*Madre de Dios*, you kick mud in my face all the way down."

"You and your greaser tripe," said Slaughter sullenly, taking half the mug of whiskey in one gulp. "I've never seen you come through yet with something from below the border. Why don't you get smart?" He slammed the cup on the bar. "Fill it again, Katz."

"On me," Rickett told the man, from behind.

Slaughter wheeled sharply. The short, curly-headed man stood there with that facile smile pinned on his face. He had changed his string tie for a flowered cravat and his Prince Albert for a maroon fustian. Slaughter spotted Thibodaux beyond *Don* Vargas, leaning against the bar, the white part gleaming greasily through the center of his queued black hair.

Standing at Rickett's shoulder was a man taller and heavier than Slaughter, his curly mat of red hair burned almost gold on the top by the sun, his short, hoary beard turned almost black across the bottom from constant contact with a red wool shirt that didn't look as if it had ever been washed. He had a Navy Colt stuck nakedly through his belt, and his muddy boots had flat heels.

"Still jayhawking, Jared?" said Slaughter sarcastically.

"Better'n letting my friends die in the river," said Jared Thorne, revealing battered, chipped teeth with his broad grin.

The dull flush crept clear to the roots of Slaughter's hair, but it was Rickett who spoke, that bland smile curling his mouth.

"We heard how you almost had a mill. It would have been too bad to lose so many fine cattle. If that cook of yours hadn't stopped it, the whole herd might well have drowned."

The memory of it cut Slaughter like a knife. Guy Bedar, with that *golondrino*. He hadn't connected it. *Guy Bedar*. He bent toward Rickett, the bunching jaw muscles filling out down into his neck until the two great muscles there stood out thickly as dally ropes.

"You . . . ," he said gutturally, "you had Bedar do that!"

Rickett smiled blandly. "The story's all over, Bob. Must be two or three trail herds camped along the river, and they've all heard it by now. First the Caverango Kid, now Solo Sam. Who do you think the cook will get on his side next?"

Slaughter's fists began opening and closing at his sides. The fumes of that bourbon were beginning to fill

111

his head now. Rickett let his glance move to Thibodaux, then back to Slaughter.

"How does it feel to lose control over your crew?" asked Rickett. "Every man in those other trail herds knows what your men think of you."

"The hell they do," said Slaughter, his guttural voice rising higher. "My men don't think any different than they did on the other side of the river. I'm not losing control over anything. But if you keep riding this horse, I will."

Rickett spread his hands. "Take it easy, Slaughter. I'm just trying to show you what's happening. The river was just the beginning. That cook won't be around to pull out your bacon every time. Jared here says there's Indian trouble farther north."

"And jayhawker trouble?" asked Slaughter.

That broad grin brought half-moon creases about the corners of Jared Thorne's mouth. "Lots of rough characters up around the Canadian River, Slaughter. Some small herd tried to beat you through to Dodge. Got cut up so bad they turned back."

"Oh, quit dragging it around outside the corral like this," said Slaughter, suddenly disgusted with the whole thing. "Get out. Get away from me."

He saw the puzzled light in *Don* Vargas's eyes as he turned back to the bar, reaching for the mug Katz had refilled. Then he felt Rickett's body brush him as the man moved in beside him.

"You don't seem to get the point, Slaughter. If the cook doesn't get the whole crew away from you and finally get your job, something else can happen. All the way up to Dodge it can happen. That river was only an illustration. On the other hand, if you do what I suggested before, we can take care of Pothooks Marrs with appalling ease. And we can see that nothing happens otherwise."

"Rickett," said Slaughter with terrible restraint, "if you don't leave me right now, I'm going to clean up this room with you."

"Now, don't be like that, Slaughter . . ."

"Damn you!" yelled Slaughter, and let all the gathered venom of this day spill out as he whirled with the mug in his hand at the end of his outstretched arm. It came around and hit Rickett fully in the face, knocking him down the bar into *Don* Vargas. Slaughter saw Jared Thorne move, and jumped on down the bar for Rickett again. Thorne had driven for him, and could not stop himself from crashing into the bar where Slaughter had stood. *Don* Vargas had turned to grapple with Thibodaux, preventing him from drawing his weapon. It gave Slaughter a chance to get Rickett again before the man could fully recover.

He grabbed Rickett by the front of his coat and heaved him across the room into a table, roaring wildly. Cowhands jumped back, upsetting their chairs, as the table overturned beneath Rickett. Slaughter jumped across at him again, bringing his fist around in a savage haymaker that caught Rickett in the face and knocked him back the other way.

Coming toward Slaughter, Thorne had to dodge aside to avoid being carried back into the bar by

Rickett. Then Rickett struck the bar with a great *thud*. His sharp, broken cry pierced the room.

Thorne was charging for Slaughter. Slaughter met him with an eager shout, blocking Thorne's clumsy blow with his right, bringing his left into the man's belly with all the animal strength of him. The force of the blow, coupled with Thorne's oncoming impetus, drove Slaughter's arm right into his shoulder until he thought it had been torn out of joint. It only stopped the man's charge part way, and Slaughter was carried backward, almost falling over the upturned table, until his back came up against the wall, with Thorne against him. The man was still sick with that blow, and could not stop Slaughter from shoving him away and striking again. It was in the belly again, and Thorne bent over the blow with a ghastly sound. It put the back of his neck to Slaughter, and the trail boss dropped a fist like a hammer there. Thorne went on down to the floor. Slaughter drew back his foot and kicked him as hard as he could in the face.

Then he turned from the man to see that Thibodaux had thrown *Don* Vargas off toward the door. The Mexican had stumbled on spike heels to the door frame, catching himself there, and trying to draw his gun. But the hammer caught on his fancy silver belt, hanging up, and all his jerking would not pull it free.

"Roberto!" he bleated.

"Never mind," panted Slaughter. "I got his number."

Thibodaux wheeled to face him. For one instant suspended in time they hung there, staring at each other, both men inclined forward slightly, both with

114

their elbows hooked out a little. After the bedlam of crashing furniture and shouting men, the abrupt silence filling the untidy room was startling.

Rickett stood against the bar, holding himself up by one elbow, dabbing at the blood covering his face in a weak, irrelevant way. The breath came out of him in a sobbing wheeze. He seemed to become aware of them, and raised himself up slightly, staring from Thibodaux to Slaughter. He did not try to hide the ruthless malice in his eyes. His lips curled in that smile with some effort, but it held no humor. It held a brutal, savage vindication. Perhaps it was what the Creole had been waiting for.

"All right, Thibodaux," Rickett said. "Go ahead. Kill him."

CHAPTER
NINE

The Pickle Bar was camped near enough to the Red to get its morning fogs. They steamed up out of the soggy earth and filled the timber like smoke from a forest fire. They brought a clammy chill that seemed to eat into Marrs's very bones as he rolled from his sougan beneath the chuck wagon. From force of habit he checked the sourdough keg, which had stood beside his bed, unwrapping its blanket with all the tenderness of a mother with her babe. He pried off the top, cocked an ear inside, sniffed speculatively, then nodded in satisfaction. The blankets had kept it warm enough. It was working fine.

But it was all done in a bleak, distracted way, with none of the usual wry humor that came to him when he performed one of these traditional chuck-wagon rituals. For it had been a sleepless night. He was fully dressed, and the Whitneyville Walker was stuck through his belt. He knew he had finished it for himself back there at the Red, breaking up Bedar's attempt to get the cattle milling and drown them. He was waiting for Rickett to come now. He knew he should have left last night. But somehow he had not been able to. In these last days he had established a bond with the Pickle Bar and the men, and it could not be broken so simply. He understood part of it. This was the first time he had not been alone in many years. The first time he could identify himself with other men, battle with them, laugh with them, see them becoming his friends, one by one. It was a precious thing to him, after so many years of loneliness. It was what he had missed most during all that time. He couldn't walk away from it so easily. It had tortured him all night long, knowing the chance he was taking. Yet he hadn't been able to leave. He wouldn't be able to leave until he actually saw Harry Rickett riding into camp, going to Kettle or Gail, telling them. Then, he knew, it would be over.

But maybe he would get to cook a last breakfast for the crew. It was the least a man could ask, when it was all he had left.

He saw the fires already going, and the Caverango Kid setting up the Dutch ovens. It was usual for the wrangler to act as swamper for the cook, when he wasn't herding the spare animals. But there was something special, something almost worshipful about the way the Kid showed up every morning, after checking the hobbled horses, to marvel at Marrs's culinary skill.

Marrs went over to the let-down lid of the wagon and started making dough, rolling it out to proper thickness with a beer bottle. Then he got four pie tins and lined their bottoms, dumping dried apples into them. After putting on the upper crust, he carved a Pickle Bar into each one with his Barlow knife. The

Kid was hunkered by one of the fires, stirring it idly with a stick, his eyes on those square, hairy hands all the time.

"Pie," he wanted to know, "for breakfast?"

"I thought you come from Texas," said Marrs.

"I do," said the Kid. "We had it at home for breakfast. But never on the trail. Slaughter told the last cook . . ."

"Where is Slaughter?" asked Marrs, glancing over at the man's empty sougan.

"Went to the Station House last night," said Waco, coming up with both hands on his belly. "He always does that when something gets his goat. I don't see how he throws a drunk like that and then comes back and puts in the kind of day's work he does. It would kill an ordinary man."

"He'll burn himself out sooner or later," said Marrs. "Your belly hurting?"

"Like hell," Waco told him. "Where's that paregoric?"

Marrs reached into the shelf holding assorted bottles of medicine. When he upended the paregoric into a tin cup, only a couple of drops leaked out.

"What the hell did you do with it?" said Waco caustically. "There was plenty left when I took it last time." He did not miss Marrs's aborted glance toward the linchpin, and began to curse viciously. "I might've known. Helluva doctor you are. That Butler don't need it any more than you do. You knew that. Why did you give it to him anyway?"

Marrs's eyes squinted. "I didn't."

"Don't try and lie out of it," berated the man viciously. "Of all the low-down, ornery, snaky things to do, that's the worst. I ought to take my pistol to you."

"Now, wait a minute," said Marrs. "What kind of hurt is it?"

"What does it matter?" said Waco, starting to turn away.

Marrs grabbed him by the arm, spinning him back against the wagon with such force it knocked a pile of plates off the chuck-box lid. "What kind of hurt is it?" he snarled. "A post oak swipe you across the belly?"

The man's pinched face held a dazed surprise. "Yeah. Let go. The doc said it probably bruised my intestines."

"You stay right here," said Marrs. "Move a step and I'll take that machete to you."

"What the hell?"

Turning away, Marrs got a can of tallow he used for lard. He poured this into the frying pan and set it over one of the fires. Then he got the blackstrap sorghum and filled a tin cup partway up with this. When the tallow was sizzling and melted, he poured it into the sorghum, and finally added a little powdered alum from the medicine chest.

"Let that cool, and down it," he told Waco. "I've seen my ma give it to more than one brush hand with his guts hurt like yours."

"That alum will burn hell out of me if there's an open sore down there," muttered the man.

"You use it to treat proud flesh on a rope burn, don't you?" said Marrs. "And then the burn heals right up.

119

That tallow and blackstrap will keep it from hurting. They'll line your guts all the way down. You'll be surprised how soothing it is."

"I never saw such a gazabo," said Waco, staring into the cup, still unconvinced. "One minute he's beating your head in, the next he's mothering you like an old hen with her chicks."

Marrs finished cooking and beat on a wreck pan with a running iron, shouting for them to come and get it. Yawning, rubbing sleep from their eyes, they appeared to get their plates and tools.

"Well," observed Pata Pala, looking at the pie, "boggy top. If it has as much soda in it as them hot rocks last night, I'll be yellow as jaundice."

"You don't need soda to get that color," Marrs told him.

"Don't get oily," flushed the peg-legged man. "I'll punch holes in your skull with my shovel leg."

"Reminds me of what Sluefoot Sue looked like after Pecos Bill got through shooting her out of the clouds," said Windy.

"Put a hobble on your jaw," Pata Pala growled. "I'm tired of hearing you blow."

"Why don't you let him finish," said Marrs. "I never heard him tell a story through yet."

Windy looked gratefully at Marrs. "Sure thing. Pecos Bill had a hoss named Widow Maker. Nobody else had ever rid the beast. When he proposed to Sluefoot Sue . . ."

"Man at the pot!" shouted Pata Pala, as Solo Sam got up to pour himself another cup of coffee. "Man at the pot!"

120

"You'll get your java when Windy finishes the story!" shouted Marrs, angered by the man's insistence.

"I'll get it or dump this bacon."

"Dump that bacon and I'll dump this coffee right on your head!"

Pata Pala turned over his plate. Marrs grabbed the three-gallon coffee pot and upended it on Pata Pala's head. The scalding, inky brew spewed out over the peg-legged man's shoulders. He danced away, his screams muffled by the pot over his head. Marrs scooped up the running iron and followed him, tripping him backward so that he fell in a sitting position against the wheel of the chuck wagon.

When Pata Pala made an effort to rise and get the pot off his head, Marrs struck the top of it with the running iron. It made a *clanging* sound. Pata Pala stiffened, dropping his hands quickly.

"Now, you finish your story," Marrs told Windy.

The white-headed old man gaped at Pata Pala, as if unable to believe his eyes. Finally he gulped, his Adam's apple bobbing like a cork in his scrawny neck. He looked around at the other men, almost fearfully. When none protested, he resumed hesitantly. "Well," began Windy, "Sluefoot said she'd marry Pecos if he let her ride Widow Maker. When Sluefoot got on, the hoss bucked the old gal so high she went through a thunderhead and it started raining. That's what caused the flood of 'Fifty-Nine."

Pata Pala made another effort to take off the pot. That iron *clanged* on its top once more. Pata Pala subsided.

"Sluefoot had some of them new-fangled hoop skirts on, and them steel hoops was just like springs every time she hit, bouncing her right back up. She went so high nobody could git her down. Pecos finally had to shoot her down to keep her from starving to death." Windy shook his head from side to side, grinning foolishly. Then a vague surprise filled his wizened face, and he stared around at them. "Well, I did finish, didn't I?" He looked at Marrs with the shining eyes of a starving dog fed a bone. "You know, Pothooks, that's the first time these jaspers let me tell one clear through since I signed on to Pickle Bar."

A quick, gleaming smile crossed Marrs's face like a flutter of light in a shadowed pool. The kindling lights filled his eyes, and for a moment they made a different man of him. Then they were gone, as swiftly as they had come. He bent to lift the pot off Pata Pala's head. Rubbing his wet, sooty head, winking coffee grounds out of his eyes, the peg-legged man jumped to his feet with a roar. He made such a ludicrous picture that the crew burst out laughing. He glared around at them.

"You got the best of it this time and you might as well admit it!" Solo Sam shouted.

A grin started at the corners of Pata Pala's mouth, and he could not control it. Pretty soon the chuckles began to shake his beefy gut. He looked down at the coffee pot, reaching up with a little finger to clean coffee grounds out of his ear.

"I guess you're right," he said, and started to go on, but the sight of something beyond the wagons halted him, his mouth still partly open. *Don* Vargas was coming in with Bob Slaughter slung across the buckskin Quarter horse, head dangling on one side, heels on the other. The whole crew gathered around as soon as the Mexican halted the animals.

"Is he dead?" asked the Caverango Kid in hushed awe.

"Only from drink," said *Don* Vargas. "He drank up all the rot-gut in the Station House last night and wrecked the place. I been dodging through the blackjack ever since with him like this. I was afraid to bring him back to camp for fear the soldiers would be here. There was a whole troop of them from Fort Sill stationed on the river, and they're all looking for Slaughter."

"Not just for cleaning out the Station House?" said Marrs.

"No," *Don* Vargas told him. "He got drunk and wrecked everything after he killed Thibodaux. The soldiers want him for murder."

The uproar of breaking camp filled the blackjack. Pots and pans *rattled* as Pothooks threw his cooking gear into the chuck box and kicked the fires out. Horses whinnied and rigging *creaked* as men saddled up, shouting to each other. Kettle Cory and Guy Bedar were already out, getting the cattle up off their bed ground, and the low bawling of the beeves formed a monotonous undertone to other sounds. *Don* Vargas and Pata Pala were alternately pouring the last of the coffee down Slaughter and dunking his head in a pail of river water in an effort to bring him out of the stupor.

123

Hearing a stir behind the chuck wagon, Marrs went back that way to find Gail Butler standing by the tailgate, taffy hair done up in a chignon, a strained look to her face.

"Have you got any other medicine *besides* the paregoric?" she said. "Paul's feeling bad again."

"What do you mean besides the paregoric?" asked Marrs.

"Waco needs that," she told him. "It's the only thing that will help him."

The restrained bitterness in his face must have reached her then, and her attention was drawn to the bottle still resting on the lid of the chuck box where Marrs had left it. She picked it up and shook it hard.

"Did Waco use it up?" she asked.

"No," said Marrs. "He was in a lot of pain."

She held out her hand in spasmodic reaction. "Pothooks, you don't think that I . . . ?" Then she broke off, her eyes losing their focus for an instant, to widen in the shock of some obscure understanding. Then they squinted, and the flush of shame crept up her neck. The whole misjudgment he had made struck him then, and he felt like a fool.

"Look," he said, "I'm sorry . . ."

"*You're* sorry," she said, pulling herself up. "What for? Getting it in the neck from Waco when he thought you'd given me the medicine? I imagine he can be very acid, can't he? I won't even apologize for that, Pothooks. Paul's my husband. If he's sick, I'm going to do whatever is necessary to help him . . ."

124

"Don't defend him, Gail," said Marrs. "He isn't worth it. You were ashamed a minute ago. It wasn't for yourself. If you'd gotten that paregoric, you would have the courage of your convictions. It was Paul who got it. More for spite than anything else. Wasn't it?"

She faced him a moment longer, deep bosom filling the crinoline with the heavy breath she took in. Then all the sand drained out of her. Her eyes dropped from him. She made a small, choked sound, as if trying to keep from crying, and began to turn away. He caught her arm.

"Don't even be ashamed of him," he said. "You and I are the only ones who will ever know this." She turned back to him, eyes meeting his in a wide, stricken need for something. "It's been this way a long time, hasn't it?" he said. The unaffected simplicity of his sympathy must have been what broke through her last reserve. She leaned forward till her face almost touched his chest, speaking in a muffled, desperate way.

"I shouldn't say things like that, I shouldn't blame Paul. He's really sick, Pothooks. A man isn't normal when he's sick. He isn't this way all the time. He was a wonderful person once, and it still comes through, when he's feeling well. It gets me down sometimes, but I can't let myself blame him."

"Don't you think you're just fooling yourself?" he said. "Loyalty and faith can be carried only so far. There's a point where they both become nothing but blindness."

She shook her head, squinting her eyes shut against the tears. "No. You're wrong, you're wrong."

He tightened his hands on her arms, seeing how tortured she was. Perhaps he had struck a truth she wasn't prepared to face yet. Or perhaps he was letting his own attraction to her prejudice him against Paul Butler.

"Forget I said it," he told her. "Time comes when we all need a kick in the pants to help us over the fence. Maybe that's all Paul needs. You say the word and I'll give it to him."

She looked at him to see that kindling of little lights in his eyes, lending his face so much humor and kindliness without the help of a smile. She tried to laugh through her tears, getting a handkerchief from her bodice to wipe her eyes. She shook her head from side to side.

"I can't reconcile it," she said.

"What?"

"In you," she said. "This kindness, this understanding and . . ."

"The way I ride the men?" he asked. "They wouldn't believe I was a cook unless I was ornery once in a while. It's what flavors the meat."

"No," she said. "I don't mean that."

"What do you mean?"

All the hesitant humor was gone from her again, and her eyes were dark. She seemed to speak with an effort. "Before we crossed the Red, Pothooks . . . after I talked with Windy . . . I was going to fire you. I couldn't bring myself to turn you in, not after you saved the Caverango Kid, but I wasn't going to have you on my crew, I couldn't. And then when you pulled Sam out of the river that way . . ." She made a defeated gesture with her hand. "I . . . I just couldn't bring myself to fire you."

Before they could go on, Bob Slaughter lurched around the end of the chuck wagon, his yellow hair still dripping, to throw his cup in the wreck pan. It made a loud *clatter* in the abrupt silence. Marrs realized for the first time how close he had been holding Gail, with one arm about her waist. For a moment, just before Slaughter spoke, he was acutely aware of the scented softness of her body, and its effect on him. He pulled away.

"Having a little tête-à-tête?" asked Slaughter sarcastically.

"That killing is going to cause Missus Butler a lot of trouble," said Marrs. "I don't think you have a right to any sarcasm."

Slaughter's eyes were bloodshot, his face puffy. "That's just it . . . Missus Butler. Did you forget she was a married woman?"

"That sounds ironic, coming from you," Gail told him caustically. Then the tone of her voice changed. "Bob, you don't understand . . ."

"I think I do," he said bitterly. "What I offered you was honest compared with" — his lips twisted on the word — "this."

Marrs let his head sink into his shoulders, lowering it slightly to stare at Slaughter. "Do you want to apologize to Missus Butler?"

"I don't think it's necessary," said Slaughter.

"Maybe I better make it necessary," Marrs told him.

"Pothooks!" cried Gail, and then *Don* Vargas stopped the whole thing by swinging in on his black and speaking loudly to Slaughter.

"What are you wasting time for, Roberto? If those soldiers don't hit our camp soon, Jared Thorne will."

Gail's head jerked upward. "Thorne was there?"

Marrs stared at *Don* Vargas, then snapped around to Slaughter again. "Why didn't you say so? If his jayhawkers are around here, this trail through the blackjack is the worst route in the world to follow. They can jump us from timber within fifty feet of the cattle on either side. Why don't you turn west along the river till the country opens up?"

"No cook is driving my cattle," said Slaughter.

Solo Sam had saddled his day horse and brought it over toward them. "He's right, Bob. No use taking more chances than need be."

"We're driving those cattle the way I started them," said Slaughter, his voice growing louder.

"And letting your men in for a nice ride to hell on a shutter anytime Jared Thorne so chooses," said Marrs. "Is that the way you figure?"

"I figure if a man hasn't got enough sand to follow where the boss leads, he shouldn't have signed up for a job like this in the first place."

"Yeah," said Marrs. "I gathered that on the Red. It isn't the men that count. It's your reputation, most of all."

Slaughter's jaw muscles began to jump and bulge beneath the stubble of blond hair. "You'd better get up

128

on your chuck wagon, Pothooks, before I tromp on you."

"Or maybe it's more than your rep," said Marrs. "This blackjack route heads eastward, doesn't it? Toward Ellsworth. Was Rickett there with Thibodaux? Did he want you to drive the cattle to Ellsworth instead of Dodge?"

Slaughter inclined his heavy torso forward in a sharp spasm. "Pothooks, I told you to . . ."

"Why should Rickett want that?" broke in Gail. "What is this, Pothooks?"

"The gambling faction in Ellsworth stands to go smash if no cattle go in there this year," said Marrs. "What do you think would happen if Slaughter broke through the sodbusters and defied that quarantine law and eventually got to Ellsworth?"

Gail looked toward Slaughter with narrowing eyes. "Most of the other trail herders would follow his lead. They usually do." She shook her head vaguely, lines knitting into her brow. "You didn't, Slaughter. You wouldn't . . ."

"Nobody's ever questioned my loyalty to the brand I work for," said Slaughter, shaking with anger.

"Maybe it's about time they did," said Marrs.

Slaughter made a spasmodic shift toward Marrs, fists clamping shut. But something held him, perhaps a realization that this was something he could not remove by merely whipping Marrs. Slaughter was a man to stand on his own feet, and Marrs had never seen him look elsewhere for reassurance before. But now, as if his direct, brutal nature were incapable of fully coping with this, he could not seem to help the movement of his eyes toward the others.

Windy met the gaze for a moment, then dropped his own eyes uncomfortably. The open animosity in Solo Sam's face caused Slaughter to drag in a deep breath. Pata Pala's blank expression gave him no support; it held a blank reserve, as if the peg-legged man were withholding a judgment.

"I'm not speaking for anything but the men," said Marrs. "If Thorne means to attack, you should move into open country for their sake."

"This blackjack route is shorter," said Slaughter. "No jayhawker is making me backtrack. Get on your horses and lift that herd off the bed ground."

The men shifted uncertainly, none of them making a move to mount. Slaughter stared at their sullen suspicion, and his voice raised to almost a shout. "You do think I sold out to Rickett! That's what's in your minds, isn't it?" He faced violently back toward Marrs. "I didn't, damn you, I didn't."

"Prove it, then," said Marrs.

"I don't have to prove it!" bawled Slaughter. He jumped for Solo Sam, catching his arm and spinning him toward his horse.

"I gave an order. Get on your horse and ride those cattle."

It wheeled Sam in against his animal, and he had to grab a stirrup leather to keep from falling. He stood there, refusing to mount, a sullen defiance on his face.

"You can whip a crew all the way from the Gulf to Canada, Slaughter," Marrs said. "But when the chips

130

re down, it takes more than that to make them follow you."

Slaughter whirled back to the cook. "Tell them I didn't sell out. That's why I shot Thibodaux. Rickett was trying to force me into it. Tell them, damn you . . ."

"I wasn't there," said Marrs.

"You're the one causing this!" said Slaughter. He had been shouting and breathing so hard his whole torso pumped like a blowing horse. Now, suddenly, the movement of breath stopped lifting his great chest, and his voice lowered to an awesome guttural. There was murder in his eyes. He moved to Marrs, taking three steps that put him close enough to reach out and grab the man. "Now tell them," he said. "Take that back, Pothooks. My guns are still with Pickle Bar and you know it. Take that back or I'll kill you."

"Bob," gasped Gail.

Anger lowered those thick lids over Marrs's black eyes, giving them that sulking sensuous look, and he contained himself with an effort so great his whole frame began trembling. "All you have to do is change the route, Slaughter."

"I'm not taking my orders from any greasy grub-spoiler!"

"Then take them from me," said Gail in what was obviously a last effort to prevent what she saw coming. "I think Pothooks is right . . ."

"Take it back, Pothooks," said Slaughter, as if he hadn't even heard Gail, giving a vicious jerk on the cook's shirt that pulled Pothooks off balance. "I didn't sell out to Rickett and you know . . ."

"I'm taking nothing back!" Marrs bawled, grabbing Slaughter's hands and tearing them free. Slaughter shouted hoarsely, his whole massive body whipping around with the punch he threw at Marrs. The cook ducked in under the blow. He put his head into Slaughter's belly like a butting bull, knocking the big, blond trail boss back against the chuck wagon so hard the wreck pan slid off the lid and dirty dishes spilled with a *clatter* all over the ground.

Slaughter caught Marrs's chin with both hands and flipped him up with such force that the cook's feet came off the ground. While Marrs was still straightened up, Slaughter hit him in the stomach. This doubled Marrs over, blinding him for a moment with the intense pain. He felt a blow lift his head again, in a shocking, jarring way, and then there was a pounding force across his back, and he knew, in the dim recesses of his consciousness, that he had struck the ground.

He rolled over and came to his feet blindly. He sensed Slaughter's rush at him and dodged aside, taking a glancing blow on the head. He caught at Slaughter's arm before the man could pull it back. Realizing his grip was on the wrist, he put his other hand on the elbow. Slaughter tried to hit him with the other fist, but Marrs twisted the arm in a swift, vicious lever, swinging around Slaughter's side at the same time and into his back with a hammer lock.

Before Slaughter could break it, with his towering strength, Marrs jammed up on the arm, forcing him to bend over, and then put all his weight against the man. Slaughter could not keep his face from going into the

132

side of the chuck wagon. Gail let out a small scream at the sickening sound it made. The very intensity of the pain gave Slaughter's spasmodic struggle to free himself a violence that tore the arm from Marrs's hammer lock.

As Slaughter swung around, pawing blood from his face, Marrs hit him again. It knocked Slaughter's head aside with such a sharp jerk Marrs thought the man's neck was broken.

Slaughter dazedly blocked the next blow with an upflung arm, and then threw himself at Marrs. Marrs blocked and counter-punched, catching Slaughter in the belly. Slaughter took it with a sick grunt, and caught Marrs with a wild haymaker. It put the cook off balance enough for Slaughter to hit him fully in the face. This knocked Marrs back, and Slaughter kept hitting him, keeping him off balance, knocking him back and back and back. Few men could have remained erect under any one of the blows. But with each one, Marrs let out a stubborn, grunting, animal sound of pain, stumbling back only so far as the blow knocked him, and there trying to regain enough balance to catch Slaughter.

Slaughter backed him all the way across camp, stumbling through gear and sougans, until Marrs finally reached him with a blind punch. It gave the cook time to set himself, and, when Slaughter tried to return the blow, Marrs blocked it, and ducked in under, to start slugging. They stood toe to toe, meting out punishment that would have finished most men in a few seconds, slugging and grunting like a couple of bulls with locked horns.

Slaughter was bigger and heavier than Marrs, possibly stronger. But in all the fights Marrs had seen the man in, in all the battles he had heard about, the trail boss had never been forced to go his limit. Slaughter's immense, driving strength had always allowed him to finish it up, quick and fast and flashy. Now in Marrs's mind was a grim resolve to outlast Slaughter. Even now the man's flash was gone. It had settled down to the horse with the most bottom. It had become a test of endurance. The very tenacity that Marrs had shown with the cattle mill on the Red was coming out in him again. Like a sullen unyielding little bull he stood there, taking all Slaughter could dish out, and giving it right back.

As if sensing the man's intent, Slaughter made an effort to end it quickly, stepping back to draw in a great breath and force Marrs to take the offensive momentarily. Marrs did, with a stolid, unhurried eagerness, moving on it. Slaughter blocked his hook, stepping in to put all his weight and strength into the blow at Marrs's belly. Marrs could not avoid it, and the punch bent him over.

For one instant the back of Marrs's neck was exposed. Slaughter lifted his fist for the famous hammer blow that had ended his fights so many times before. But as it came down, Marrs thrust his whole weight into Slaughter. His head was against Slaughter's belly and his arms about the man's hips when Slaughter's fist hit his neck. The gasp erupted from Marrs in a explosion, but he was already driving with his legs. He shoved Slaughter backward. Stunned by the blow, Marrs nevertheless kept pushing. He felt another blow on his neck, but Slaughter was off balance, still stumbling backward, and it lacked its former force. Then they came up against the chuck wagon again.

Marrs straightened, moving back far enough to slug Slaughter in the belly. Slaughter tried to keep himself straight and meet it. Again that awful slugging match began, Slaughter pinned in against the wagon, unable to avoid it. All he could do was meet Marrs blow for blow. He was tiring. His sounds, his movements, the ghastly, fixed, bloody expression on his face — all gave him away.

Marrs felt the slackening, and summoned the last concentrated force in him, catching Slaughter on the jaw with a blow. It knocked Slaughter around till he was facing down the wagon. Marrs hit him again, solidly, terribly, grunting with the awful effort. Slaughter slid down the wagon box. He tried to keep his knees from buckling, tried to drive up again. Marrs hit him once more. Slaughter made a sick, defeated sound, and sank to the ground, rolling over on his belly.

Black hair down over his eyes, shirt torn from his heavy torso, blood and sweat dribbling off his face, Marrs took one step and caught the side of the wagon to keep himself from falling. Chest heaving, he stared dazedly down at the trail boss. Then a whooping roar filled his ears. The whole crew crowded around him, slapping him on the back, yelling and congratulating him.

They half carried him to the water butt and soused it all over him, washing off the blood. Grinning feebly, he tried in a half-hearted way to shove them off. They would have none of it. Solo Sam tore the ruined shirt off and went and got one of his own. Windy pulled a bottle of rot-gut from his sougan and tilted it up at Marrs's mouth.

The fiery liquor cleared Marrs's head. He realized he was trembling. Then the jubilance died down.

Slaughter had pulled himself erect. He looked them over, one by one, and on his face Marrs saw that it was not in the man to stay and rod a crew where he had been whipped by one of them. Finally he turned his great bleeding frame and dragged it along the wagon to the end of the box. From there to his horse, he fell twice. It was painful, watching him drag himself onto the animal. Marrs thought he had never seen such a defeated man.

But Slaughter reined the Quarter horse around and brought it back. He sat slackly in the saddle, looking down at Marrs, holding the horn to keep from falling off. Each breath he sucked in seemed to cause him painful effort, making a gusty, wheezing sound. He moved his cut and mashed lips, trying to say something, but at first no words would come. Finally he managed to get it out, in a voice that sounded more animal than human.

"The next time I see you, Marrs, I'm going to kill you."

CHAPTER
TEN

The morning sun was eating through the fog now, cutting it into misty shreds that wound through the timber like tattered streamers. The cattle were bawling plaintively in the deep spring grass, shifting restlessly about despite the crooning of the circle riders. It was as if the herd felt the tension, the indecision that had settled over the whole crew.

Gail Butler stood by the chuck wagon, watching the men roll their sougans and saddle up. She watched Pata Pala swing his wooden leg over his horse and settle his bulk in the saddle. He was the strongest one of the bunch in many ways, and was the logical choice for trail boss, now that Slaughter was gone. But she knew that he had prodded Windy all the way north, and was not liked by several of the other men. Could he command their respect? She shook her head, doubting it.

Who else, then? Windy was too old, *Don* Vargas too shallow. Solo Sam was a top hand, but he wasn't the type to boss a crew. The farther she went down the list, the worse it seemed to get.

She looked up as Marrs walked back from the water butt. He had washed his face and rubbed grease into the cuts and bruises, and looked as if he felt better. He was holding one hand over his ribs, however, and seemed to feel pain when he breathed.

"Think they're broken?" she asked.

He squinted his eyes and shook his head. "Don't think so. But that man hits like the hind end of a mule."

"I've seen some fights," she said. "Never one like that."

He seemed to be studying her closely. "Trying to decide who's going to rod your crew?"

She nodded darkly. "Slaughter left a big hole, Pothooks. No matter what else he may be, he's the best trail boss in all of Texas." She sent him a narrow-eyed glance. "How did you know Rickett bribed Slaughter?"

She saw his lips grow thin. "Because Rickett tried to bribe me. He wanted me to help Bedar start that mill on the Red. He thought it might convince Slaughter that he'd better turn back to Ellsworth."

"Where did Rickett know you before?" she asked. "San Antonio?"

A savage expression made the muscles of his jaws bulge thickly. She saw defiance lower the heavy lids over his eyes. She caught his arm.

"Don't be like that. We might as well be honest with each other. I've gone along this far, knowing who you are. Windy told me about it. I told you I was ready to fire you, before you saved Solo Sam's life. But now . . ."

His voice was tight. "Now?"

"Now I find it hard to believe that a man who's befriended this crew like you have, a man who's coddled them like kids, who's risked his life for them, could . . ."

138

"Could tie a man to a mesquite tree and torture him to death?" he said in a thin voice.

"I told you not to be like that," she said. "I'm not accusing you now. I'm not condemning you. How can anyone believe a man innocent if he won't even deny his guilt?"

For a while she did not think he would answer. Finally, however, he said: "What if the man's denied his guilt a million times, and nobody ever believed him? Don't you think he gives up trying?"

She spoke softly. "You haven't tried me," she said.

Again it was a long time before he spoke. She could see him searching her face intently, almost painfully. "All right," he said at last. "I didn't tie anybody to a mesquite tree and torture him to death."

"And Gary Carson?"

His head dropped forward, a putty color filling his cheeks.

"Gary Carson and I grew up together," he said. "We even mavericked together, before he joined the San Antonio Cattlemen's Association. Everybody was mavericking in those days. Gary was the one who came out to tell me when the bill went through outlawing mavericking. I quit right then, and he knew it. That's why he talked that bunch of stock detectives out of filling the shack full of lead when they'd holed me up south of Corpus Christi. Gary knew that, if the shooting would stop and I could get out and talk, I could clear myself. He came up to the shack with that white handkerchief and I said sure I'd come out and talk. He turned around and started back to tell the rest

139

of them. Then that shot came. I guess Gary was dead before he hit the ground. I didn't do it. I couldn't have. Not Gary. Rickett and the others made a sieve of the shack in a minute. I was hit half a dozen times. I don't know how I lived through it."

She looked at his eyes, so squinted, so hurt. She tried to see his face as it had been before those years of being hunted and hounded had shaped in into that expression of bitter withdrawal.

She spoke softly. "I want to believe you," she said.

She saw hope seep into his face. His voice was husky with emotion. "I was ready to run again here. Rickett said, if I didn't help Bedar drown those cattle, he'd spread the word where I was and what I looked like now. He'd tell you and Kettle and all the others."

"At least he can't hold the part about telling me over your head," Gail said. She saw the waiting expression in his eyes, and knew what was in his mind. She touched his hand, feeling the animal warmth of it run through her. "I couldn't fire you after the Red, Pothooks, and I can't do it now. I want to believe you. I want to give you a chance. If you want to stay, you can."

She saw gratitude fill his face. Before he could say anything, however, Windy rode up.

"Them cattle is getting restless, Missus Butler. You decided what you're going to do yet?"

She looked from Marrs to the old man. "Pothooks was right about this timber, wasn't he? If those jayhawkers meant to jump us, it would give them a big advantage."

140

"Sure would. And with Slaughter out there and mad, it's even worse. I have an idea he'll join up with Thorne or Rickett and come back as soon as he can."

"Do you know the country west of here, Windy?"

"None of us do. We've gone north before, but it was always straight up the Chisholm."

She realized he was looking at Marrs. She found herself turning that way, too. Then she began to remember.

"Before the fight, you asked Slaughter why he didn't turn the herd west until the country opens up. How do you know it opens up?"

Marrs seemed hesitant. "Well," he said, "I don't know."

"Have you been there?"

"I guess so."

"You know the country. Tell me, Pothooks."

"Yes," he said with that old defensiveness. "I know it."

She found herself looking back up at Windy. The same thing was in his eyes. He spat.

"You thinkin' what I'm thinkin'?" he asked.

"I guess I am," she said.

But there were a thousand doubts in her, a million apprehensions. Windy saw them, and took off his hat to run a hand through his weedy shock of white hair.

"Well, you got to remember, Marrs took more from this crew than those other three belly cheaters took all together, and he stayed on to cook. You got to remember he took a good chance on getting killed, when he could've just stood by and watched them cattle drown in the river."

Slowly she turned back to Marrs. "Will you do it?"

He frowned, as if finding it hard to believe. "Are you talking about a trail boss?"

"We need one."

He took a deep breath. "Yes," he said. "I'll do it."

Windy cackled and slapped his leg. "That's prime, that's real prime." Then he sobered again. "But who's going to cook?"

"I'll cook," Marrs said. "I'll cook and I'll drive your cattle, too. Now come on. Let's get them on the road."

CHAPTER
ELEVEN

The first thing Marrs wanted to do was get rid of Bedar. Gail agreed with him that it would be better to run short-handed than to take a chance on having the man betray them again. But they could not find him. The Caverango Kid said he had seen the man riding eastward into timber, and had assumed he was after a stray. But Marrs knew he was after no stray. The man had obviously known he was through as soon as Gail made Marrs trail boss, and had not waited to be fired.

Marrs hated to take another man off the herd, but he could not do much work from the chuck wagon, so he asked Windy to drive the outfit. The old man consented reluctantly, grumbling that a hand had really reached the end of his rope when he herded cows on four wheels. Before they started, Marrs took the five-pound sourdough keg from the chuck wagon and lashed it on behind his saddle. This drew a shrill cackle from Windy.

"I didn't think you'd trust that barrel o' gold to anybody else," he said.

"Not even my own mother," Marrs said, slapping the keg.

"Wouldn't be no use going on if we lost this."

And then they started. They rode west until they reached the Red, driving fast and hard through the damp clumps of willow and post oak and hackberry that stood deep in the viscid mud of the bottom lands. In the late afternoon they left the timber and turned north into hills that rolled away against the horizon like billows of mauve smoke. They camped in a shallow bunch-grass valley and Marrs cooked the evening meal. He was played out from the double duty, and turned in early. He unrolled his sougan beneath the chuck wagon, placed his six-gun by his side, and folded a saddle blanket over the sourdough keg. But thoughts of Slaughter out there somewhere would not let him sleep, and finally he crawled out to relieve *Don* Vargas on the graveyard, riding his restlessness out on the herd.

And the second day. The restless sea of jade-green hills unfolding endlessly into the misty horizon. One thousand steers beating up dust from the land to lie against the skyline like mealy gold. The plaintive bawl of a tired beef and the muffled nicker of a horse and the wavering voice of Solo Sam coming out of nowhere and dying again in the vastness:

> *I'll get me a Porter saddle*
> *And a line-back bronco to boot . . .*

Near noon Marrs scouted a big circle around the herd, finding no sign of jayhawkers, and then returned to take the chuck wagon over from Windy and drive ahead a mile with Kettle Cory scouting till they found good grounds for the noon halt. They unhitched the

144

mules in the shade of a lone hackberry and tethered them to a rope line. Kettle collected buffalo chips for the fire. They had butchered a beef the day before, and from this Marrs cut his steaks, salting them down, and dousing them with garlic.

By the time he had finished this, the fire was working to his liking. He filled the coffee pot with water Kettle had drawn from the brackish sink by the tree, and dumped in a pound of Triple X. He set it on the ground and got a shovel full of coals from the fire to bank up around the pot's windward side. Kettle put the big sheet of corrugated iron on the ground for him, and Marrs spread a layer of hot coals on it. Upon these he put the three skillets to heat. From the sourdough keg he scooped a rough pound of fermented dough, replacing it with the same amount of flour and adding salt and water, so it would be working for the next day. He rolled the dough out on the tailboard, paper-thin, skillet-size. All the time he was working, he felt Kettle's eyes on him, and he was filled with an ever-growing tension. Stiffly he put the dough in the first skillet, placed a smaller sheet of iron on top, piled hot coals on it. As he straightened, Kettle chuckled huskily.

"I never saw a man like you. What's the sense of building a fire if you never use it?"

"No pothooks worth his salt cooks over the flames."

"Last cook did."

"And you threw him out the second day."

The man grinned, wiping at his sweaty face. "I guess we did."

Marrs frowned at him. "Your own little joke?"

Kettle's great gut trembled with his deep chuckle. "All right. Don't you think I've et in enough cow camps to know how they cook? What do you think we was all watching for, that first meal you threw together for the Pickle Bar? You didn't use the fire for nothing but making coals to cook with. We all knew you was the real potatoes right then."

"You picked a funny way of showing it."

"Well . . ." Kettle took out the mashed chunk of lead he was always flipping, squinted at it, pursed his lips. "Maybe we was just testing you."

The man was grinning broadly. But his eyes weren't grinning. There was something speculative in their chill blue gaze, something waiting. Suddenly Marrs could stand it no longer. Kettle must know who he was. Windy had guessed it as soon as he had shown his skill with a rope. And if it was that clear to the old man, it would be doubly clear to Kettle. Marrs was through playing a game. He was going to bring it out in the open. He had to. He felt his fists clench.

"Kettle . . . ?"

That was as far as he got. The moving silhouettes on the horizon stopped him. Kettle saw his gaze change focus, and turned to look. He took a wheezing breath.

"Horsebackers," he said. "Lots of 'em."

He turned and walked over to his hairy cutting horse and pulled the Winchester from its scarred saddle boot, wheeling to squint against the sun at the riders. They were no longer silhouettes now.

"No jayhawkers this time," Kettle said.

Marrs could see that now. They were Indians. They came through a saddle and into the little valley like a file of ghosts. For the most part they were dressed in nothing but moccasins and leggings, their bare torsos shimmering like dust-covered bronze in the bright sun. Half of them had rifles across their horses' withers — old breech-loading Springfields from the war, early model Spencers, rusty bolt-action Ward-Burtons — and the rest carried short, lethal war bows. The leader kneed his pinto past the brackish sink of water by the hackberry and halted by the chuck wagon. He was tall and arrogant in his buffalo saddle, jet-black eyes glittering in a face with high cheek bones that was daubed gaudily with ocher paint. With a whisper of feathers bobbing in the wind, a muffled tremble of earth beneath unshod hoofs, the others drifted in around the first. When they had all stopped, a score of them, staring blankly at the white men, the leader spoke.

"Nipi okcha ki tushali."

"What's that?" Kettle said.

"Choctaw," Marrs told him. "They want some meat."

"Choctaw?" Kettle's squint made his little blue eyes recede into their pouches of fat till they were barely visible. "Ain't they off their reservation?"

" 'Way off. This is Chickasaw country."

"And paint on their faces. That's bad, ain't it?"

"Not necessarily." Marrs began to drop the steaks into the skillet. "Just put away that Winchester and don't make any quick moves."

"You ain't giving them steaks to these Injuns! That crew comes in and finds you without meat for 'em, they'll be ringy as horny toads in a cook fire."

"Who'd you rather have jumping down your craw . . . a ringy crew or a ringy Indian?"

Kettle wiped a fat palm across his greasy face. "And all I thought we had to worry about was Jared Thorne and his jayhawkers."

The Indians dismounted and gathered warily around the fires, holding tightly to their rifles and bows, talking gutturally in their own language. The Indian Nations made a haven for all kinds of men on the dodge, and Marrs had put in enough time there during the last years. He had learned enough Choctaw to converse, but could not follow it when they spoke among themselves this way. By the time the steaks were ready, the coffee was done. With a great *clatter* the Indians fished tin cups from the wreck pan, and Marrs poured their coffee. When he set the pot down, Kettle waddled over and picked it up, shaking it by his ear.

"Empty. Pothooks, that's too much."

He threw the pot down and whirled on the Indians. He saw one who hadn't yet drunk his coffee, and lunged for the cup. The Indian jumped back. The others spread away with surprised shouts, dropping their cups and plates and jerking up their guns. But Marrs caught Kettle's arm before he could get the coffee cup from the man.

"Slack off, Kettle. You want to start a war?"

Kettle struggled ineffectually against his hold. "Damn it, Pothooks, that's taking the breath of life

148

from a man. I've been looking forward to a cup of that Triple X all morning long."

"It's the custom. They expect gifts and such for letting us drive through their lands. You'd better quiet down if you want to keep your hair."

Glaring at the Indians, Kettle subsided with a subterranean rumble. Slowly, angrily the Indians picked up their cups and tin plates. Some had dropped their steaks in the dirt, but they put them back on the plates and began to eat them again without brushing them off. The leader was staring venomously at Kettle. His voice sounded like the whir of a rattlesnake.

"*Shukka bila.*"

"What's that?" Kettle asked.

"You just got a new name," Marrs told him.

"What is it?"

"Promise you won't be foolish again?"

"I promise."

"He called you Hog Fat."

A ruddy glow crept into Kettle's face and a pulse swelled up in his temple till Marrs thought it would burst. The fat man's voice was thick and strained.

"What's the worst thing you can say in their language?"

Marrs couldn't help it. He had to chuckle. "I won't tell you," he said. "They'd massacre us."

That subterranean rumble ran through Kettle again. "I killed a man once that made fun of my size. I took him between my thumb and forefinger and broke him into matchsticks."

149

The Indians stared intently at him, as if trying to understand what he had said, and went to jabbering among themselves again, like a bunch of gossipy old maids. When they were finished eating, they dropped the tinware on the ground and mounted their horses, blankets swirling, feathers bobbing in the wind. The leader held up a hand to Marrs.

"*Achukma wak.*"

"Good cow to you, too," Marrs told him.

Marrs choked in the dust they lifted galloping away. They were silhouetted on the first hill for a while, war bows etching their scimitar curves against the sky. Then they dropped off the hill and were out of sight. Marrs turned around to look at Kettle. In the same moment, the bawl of steers reached him, and the point rider over the low crest of a southerly hill. It was Pata Pala, on his hairy bay. It was a cutting horse, but he seemed to ride it for every job he did. He cantered ahead of the herd and checked the animal by the camp.

"Where's them steaks? You had all day."

"You'll have to butcher me another steer if you want steaks."

"Another steer? You had plenty of meat this morning. And what about that coffee?"

"Fixing."

"Fixing!" Pata Pala swung angrily off his horse, staring around the camp, a growing rage sending its rush of blood into his heavy jowls. "What the hell," he said. "You and this tub of leaf lard drunk it. You drunk the coffee and ate them steaks."

"Indians ate the steaks."

150

"Indians, hell!" Pata Pala moved toward Marrs, jabbing his peg leg viciously into the dirt with each step. "I told you I'd poke my foot through your gizzard. Now I'm goin' to do it. And no Slaughter around to break it up this time. There ain't no Indians within a hundred miles, and you know it."

"Maybe you better look up on the ridge," Kettle said.

Pata Pala started to wheel toward the fat man. Then he checked himself, staring northward. They were there. They had passed over the first crest and crossed the valley beyond. But now they were silhouetted on a farther ridge, feathers bobbing in the wind, war bows curving wickedly against the sky.

"They ain't moving," Kettle said.

"No," Marrs said. "They're watching."

The three of them stood without speaking after that, staring off at the somber silhouettes on the skyline, until the first Pickle Bar cattle began to kick the dust into the wind, passing camp, and Gail Butler pulled the linchpin to a halt beside the chuck wagon. Paul sat beside her, wrapped up in a ratty buffalo robe. She shaded her eyes with a hand to follow their gaze northward.

"Indians?" she asked.

"Choctaws."

She looked at Marrs. "Bad?"

He shook his head, frowning. "Maybe, maybe not. There's a lot of restlessness among the tribes. Rumors around that the government's going to move them again. They're sick of moving. Every time it's less land and worse land. They blame it on the cattle coming through. They think if it wasn't for that, they could stay where they are. This may be just a bunch of wild bucks jumping reservation to raid the Chickasaws for some horses."

"Or it may be a war party out to jump a trail herd," Gail said, finishing it for him. "Is that what you mean?"

He met her eyes, surprised that he should feel a pride in the unflinching way she faced trouble. "I suppose so," he said. "You want to turn back?"

"Maybe we'd better," Butler said.

"And meet Jared Thorne and his jayhawkers?" Gail asked impatiently. "The Indians have seen us now anyway, Paul. If they mean to attack, they'll do it whether we go ahead or turn back."

"But we're short-handed already."

"What do you think?" Gail asked Marrs, cutting off her husband.

"I think you're right," Marrs said. "They've seen us now. The direction we took wouldn't have much bearing on what they did."

He saw Butler start to protest again, then check himself, looking around at the other men. They were watching Butler, with a waiting, almost avid expression in their faces. Marrs saw Butler's eyes flutter with indecision, drop sullenly before their gazes. He pulled the buffalo robe around his shoulders, something petulant to the shape of his mouth.

"I was just thinking of the crew," he muttered.

Marrs searched the man's face for some sign of what Gail had originally seen in it. There was an arrogance to the high bridge and pinched nostrils of the nose; the shape of his head could have been proud if he held it higher. His dark eyes might have been handsome once, but they were sunken too deeply in their sockets now, tinged with the jaundiced color of long sickness. It made him look ten years older than Gail. And yet, Marrs wondered, was it all sickness? He had seen failure stoop a man that way, sink gaunt hollows into his face, drain all the life from his eyes. Or even the fear of failure.

Marrs saw Gail watching him. There was a plea to her parted lips, as if she were asking him not to pass too harsh judgment on the man. He turned back to his cooking.

That was a miserable meal, with the Indians silhouetted against the sky all the time, motionless, sinister, waiting. The crew dropped off duty in pairs to eat while the rest kept the herd moving by. There was only pan bread and coffee. Marrs didn't want to take time to butcher another steer. If the Choctaws were merely a raiding party, the quicker the herd was moved out of their sphere, the better. Remaining within their sight too long might only stir up underlying rancor and light flames of anger that would remain untouched if the cattle were pushed by them soon enough.

When the drag riders were out of sight in the dust of the herd, and the Caverango Kid was through eating, Marrs put the wreck pan into the wagon with the dishes still dirty and slammed up the tailgate.

"How about you driving that linchpin, Mister Butler, while Missus Butler takes this chuck outfit?" he asked. "That way Windy could go back to the herd, and we'll need every hand we can get if those Choctaws follow us."

Butler was huddled over the fire, sitting on a spare saddle, a half-filled coffee cup in one pale hand. "Don't be a fool," he said angrily. "I don't have the strength to drive those horses."

Gail turned from where she had been straightening traces in the terrets of her harnessed team. Marrs could see a conflict passing through her face. She spoke stiffly.

"You really need that extra man, don't you?"

"It might mean the difference between saving the herd and losing it, if those Indians jump us," Marrs said.

"Paul," she said. "Please."

He stood up, flinging his cup down. "What are you trying to do, kill me? I'm a sick man. I can't do it and you know it."

"Yes, you can," she said. Her face was chalky. "I'm going to drive the chuck wagon, Paul. If you don't want to be left behind, you'll have to drive the linchpin."

His mouth hung open. He stared at her as if unable to believe what he had heard. Suddenly the blood flamed into his sallow cheeks, his nostrils pinched in with waspish rage.

"Gail!"

"Do you want to make a scene, Paul?"

Her voice cut him off. It had a brittle tone, like something ready to snap with a little more pressure. She was drawn up to her full height, with a painful stiffness to her body. Butler seemed to become aware of

154

how intensely the Caverango Kid and Windy were watching. There was no sympathy in either of their faces. They looked eager, like hounds waiting for something to happen. The color in Butler's cheeks grew deeper. His eyes swung on around till they reached Marrs. They were glittering with an intense rage. His voice was thin, womanish, venomous. "You son-of-a-bitch!"

Marrs felt the violent reaction grip his body like a great fist. For an instant there was nothing in his consciousness but an urge to lunge at the man. The effort to check himself ran through him in a spasm. Finally he settled back and spoke in a voice that was thick and husky with restraint.

"You better not say that to me when you're a well man, Butler."

A flutter of muscle ran through Butler's gaunt cheeks, and he started to speak again. Before he could, Gail's voice cut him off.

"Paul," she said. "You fool . . ."

She broke off. Her eyes were almost squinted shut as she wheeled sharply and half ran to the chuck wagon. The Kid had harnessed the mules and all she had to do was climb into the seat and pick up the reins. Butler started after her, one hand held out.

"Gail!"

She didn't answer him. She took up the reins and slapped them hard against the wheelers' rumps. The mules lunged into their collars with startled grunts, and the wagon *clattered* into motion. Butler stopped, hand still held out, staring helplessly after her.

"Well." Windy grinned. "Looks like I go back to a decent job."

Marrs turned to him. "Get to it, then. You too, Kid."

Windy unhitched his horse from the hackberry, and the Kid went over to get the cavvy from *Don* Vargas, who had spelled him on watching the spare horses while he ate. Butler stood where he had stopped, not turning around. Marrs knew the man did not want to face any of them, after such humiliation. He was surprised that he felt no more anger toward Butler. He almost felt compassion. There was something so defeated and lonely about the slumped figure.

"Let's forget it, Mister Butler," Marrs said. "I was only thinking of the herd. I didn't mean to interfere in your private business."

Slowly Butler turned to him. Marrs didn't know what he had expected from the man actually. Another burst of rage, probably. He had only spoken on impulse. But the rage was gone from Butler's face. It was filled with a lost expression. It made Marrs realize this must have been the first time in a long while that Gail had bucked Butler so directly. Had it done something to the man? Made him stop and think, maybe?

"I guess there isn't another hand in the crew who would come back and say something like that, after what happened, Marrs," Butler said. "Why do you do it?"

The utter change surprised Marrs. There was something childish about it. All the violent conflicts and intense rage of a moment before seemed forgotten.

156

"Maybe the others don't understand what's going on inside you," Marrs said. "Maybe I do."

"Understand? What are you talking about?"

"You must know who I am by now."

"Lee M. Benton? I began to suspect it when Gail told me about that roping."

"And you let me stay?"

"I wasn't sure, at first. As I say, only a suspicion. And after you saved those cattle on the Red . . ." He shrugged. "How could we fire you?" He frowned at Marrs. "But what's that got to do with your understanding me?"

"Say a man's been running for fifteen years, Mister Butler. Running and hiding like an animal. Jumping at his own shadow. Hated by the men who used to be his closest friends. Betrayed by them. Hounded by every man who ever knew him. Don't you think he'd understand another man who's been running?"

"What man?"

"You, Mister Butler. The only difference is I've been running from other men, you've been running from yourself."

A startled look widened Butler's eyes. Then that reasonless rage leaped into them.

"Don't start that again," Marrs said. "You've been coming up with that every time something happened. What's it got you? What did it get you this afternoon? Missus Butler walked out on you. Why don't you stop and think a minute, Mister Butler? Why don't you look yourself square in the face and see what's really there?"

157

For a while longer he saw that anger struggling to surface in the man. But there was a great, dark confusion struggling with it. Finally Butler turned away, walking to the linchpin. He stood by the bed, back to Marrs, shoulders bowed. He reached up to rub at the back of his neck. Finally, in a low voice, he said: "Where does a man lose out, Marrs? He has everything to begin with. A beautiful woman. The biggest ranch in Texas. An army of friends. What happens along the way?"

"Maybe you haven't given yourself a chance to get well."

"Not that, Marrs. Not just sickness."

"A string of bad years can take the heart out of a man."

"Don't try to make it easy on me. Those things shouldn't get a man down for good. Maybe I didn't have any heart to begin with. Maybe that's my trouble."

Marrs leaned toward the man, surprised at himself for trying to find some excuse for him. "Don't be like that, Mister Butler. It must have taken a lot of man to attract Missus Butler in the first place. If you were like that once, you can be like it again. And it's going to take that to keep her."

The man turned, frowning up at him, indecision working at his face. Then he came over to Marrs and grasped the cook's arm. "You're right. I'm losing her. I can feel it. She's all I have. If she goes, I won't have anything left. I want to do the right thing, want to treat her the way I used to. But every time it gets twisted. I act like a fool, a child. A man gets off the track, somewhere along the way. He can't find his way back. He needs help, Pothooks. Needs a friend. I haven't got one in this whole crew, not one man to tell me what to do."

"If you're asking me," Marrs said, "you can start out by getting in that wagon and driving it up with the herd."

For a moment there was gratitude in Butler's face. It embarrassed Marrs. The man was looking at him as if he had given him a profound bit of advice, yet he could not feel that he had given him anything. Then, with that childish transition, the man's face had changed. His eyes darkened; his lower lip grew petulant. Marrs knew he was regretting having revealed himself so deeply. He wheeled to climb up into the wagon.

"All right," he said stiffly. "You can go ahead with the herd. I'll be along."

Marrs watched him a moment longer, then went to his mare, mounted, and kicked it into an easy canter. But he couldn't help wondering about Butler. He seemed such a contradiction. Raging like a child one moment, forgetting it the next. And there was something strange about a grown man who could reveal himself so suddenly and completely to a veritable stranger, turning to him as candidly and naïvely as a child. There was something pathetic about it, and something almost unwholesome. And yet he couldn't dislike the man for it. Because Butler was tortured by something. And he knew what it was to be tortured.

Then he forgot Butler, because he had passed the hackberry, and he could see the hills beyond the herd, and he remembered the Choctaws. He squinted to see through the tawny haze of dust.

They were still there.

CHAPTER
TWELVE

It was a rolling land north of the Red, a vast and rolling land, vivid with spring. The grass was knee-deep and green as jade; the Judas trees were red as blood on the hillsides; the dogwood blossoms lay like spattered cream on every slope. But Gail Butler could take no pleasure in its beauty. For they were still there.

They were there all morning long, sitting on a ridge top, their feathers bobbing in the wind, their war bows etched against the sky. Gail could not keep her gaze off them. Bumping along in the chuck wagon, fighting the willful mules, she watched until her eyes ached.

Marrs had told everybody to stick close, and Gail clung to the left flank of the herd, so close the long horns of the steers kept *clattering* against the wagon bed. Behind her, Paul was driving the linchpin. Whenever she turned to look, he raised his hand. There seemed to be no rancor in him, and that puzzled her. Had her stand finally lifted him from his spiteful misery? Or was this merely another of his unpredictable changes?

Near noon, Marrs dropped back from his point position. He passed Gail, raising a hand, and she knew he was going back to check on the Caverango Kid. He

161

looked tired, stooped a little in the saddle, and she realized what a change had occurred in him since she had first seen him back in Dallas. The hard work and long hours had melted off all the excess weight he had picked up working indoors. His waist was no longer thick and square; it had a lean, hungry look, and made his shoulders appear even broader than before. There were faint hollows beneath his blunt cheek bones, and she could see little bunches of muscle along the angle of his jaw, beneath the bluish cast of his beard. The change in him told her of the strain his double responsibility was putting on him.

He kept looking off toward the east, where there were no Indians in sight, and Gail finally guessed what was in his mind. There were more than Choctaws to worry about. There was Bob Slaughter.

A while after Marrs had disappeared in the dust of the drag, Kettle Cory came riding his hairy black cutting horse through the haze, sweat pouring down the creases of his face.

"Seen Pothooks?" he asked.

"He went to check on the Kid!" she called through the incessant sounds of *clacking* horns and bawling steers. "Seems to think the spare horses are what caught the Indians' eyes."

The man shook his head. "I've been scouting ahead. Caught sight of another bunch of Injuns. Thought Marrs had better know."

"He'll be back this way in a minute. Are you sure it isn't just a part of the first bunch?"

He spat dust from his mouth, shaking his head. "I've been watching that first bunch close. None of them left it. This is new Injuns, and I don't like it."

"It's rather odd," she said, "your going to Marrs."

He had been keeping his horse at a walk beside the chuck wagon, squinting apprehensively over his shoulder toward the rear. Now he turned sharply to look at her. She got the full effect of those disturbingly lucid little eyes, set so secretively into their pouches of fat.

"You made Marrs the boss, didn't you?" he asked.

"You know what I mean, Kettle."

"No." He drew the word out in a whispering way. "Just what do you mean?"

"How long ago did you work for the San Antonio Cattlemen's Association?"

She saw his jowl muscles bunch suddenly. His eyes closed till they were merely silvery slits between the pink lids. He studied her face a long time before he spoke.

"Ten or twelve years ago, I guess."

"About the time of the Lee M. Benton case?"

He settled his great bulk deeply in the saddle, still squinting at her. He took out his bandanna and wiped the inevitable sweat lying like grease in the crevices of his face. His breathing made a wheezing sound.

"Are you still working for the Association?" she asked.

He drew in a long, stertorous breath. His face was pink as a baby's, and he looked angry. Then he pursed his lips and let the breath out with a whistle. There was something resigned to the sound. Finally he spoke.

"I ain't an Association detective, out to get Pothooks Marrs, if that's what you mean."

"Did you recognize him?"

Now that it was in the open, some of the reluctance to talk was leaving him. "Not at first. It's amazing how much he's changed. I guess going through that kind of hell would do it for a man. When Windy told me about that roping with the Kid, though, I figured Pothooks could be no other than Lee Marrs Benton. Not many ropers that good come along in a man's lifetime."

"Why should he take his middle name like that? You'd think it would have been smarter to change it completely."

"Nobody ever knew what that M stood for. All the records only had Lee M. Benton. I've hunted lots of missing men. You'd be surprised at the dodges they pull to keep some link with the past. They never quite change their whole name. Switch it around, use the initials, use their mother's name. In this case, we'd never've added it up except for that roping."

"Marrs escaped jail. I imagine there's a bounty on his head."

Kettle shook his head. "I ain't after any reward, either."

"Then why ride him this way? Why not bring it out in the open, tell him you know who he is, tell him you're not after him. Can't you see how it's eating him?"

Kettle fished the chunk of mashed lead from his pocket and began flipping it, as he often did when thinking. "Gary Carson and that other murdered Association man were both cattle detectives, both my friends. If it had been cut and dried, I might take Marrs in right now, for their sakes. But it ain't cut and dried."

"What do you mean?" she asked.

"For instance, why should Benton's term suddenly be commuted to life imprisonment, after the jury had unanimously voted a death sentence? I talked with a lot of dubious characters along the border about that. Found out some things. You know how big a man Boa Snyder is now, and Curt Young, and Axel Murray. Them and a dozen others got their start mavericking, riding with Lee Benton before mavericking was outlawed. From another saddlemate of Benton's, I heard that after Benton had run into a couple of minor double-crosses, he figured he'd play it safe. He began to record the men he rode with, the territory they covered, the brand and earmarks they put on the mavericks, and the probable outfit those mavericks really belonged to. With mavericking now looked on as rustling, you can see what that kind of information would do to a man in public life. Especially if some of it pertained to mavericking after the practice was outlawed."

"But Pothooks claims he quit as soon as it was outlawed."

"Maybe he did. But a lot of 'em didn't. And maybe Benton was still keeping records. Do you see what dynamite he'd have?"

"What happened to it?"

"From what I could gather, Benton put the information into the hands of a lawyer, to be turned over to the proper authorities upon Benton's death. I tried to locate the lawyer, but I didn't know his name. He'd apparently realized what a dangerous thing he held, and hid out."

"Are you saying that Boa Snyder and those others were so afraid of having that information appear on Benton's death that they brought pressure to have the sentence commuted?"

"Doesn't it look that way?" Kettle asked. "I was bounced for snooping. SACA gave me the boot, and no other association would hire me."

"And you didn't tell anybody, you didn't make any attempt to . . . ?"

"To what? It didn't prove Benton's innocence in the murders. It only indicated that there was more behind the killings than appeared on the surface. And I didn't have any real proof of that. The men with enough influence to commute a death sentence like that are powerful, Missus Butler. I wouldn't want to go against them unless I had ironclad proof."

She settled back, studying him. "And that's why you're giving Pothooks the benefit of the doubt."

"It has a lot to do with my own feelings. A man can make a career of association work, just the way he can be a banker, a lawyer. Ten years I'd been with SACA. They take that away from a man, he gets mad. He says the hell with it. Give the man on the other side a break. Particularly when you see him with this crew. They're like a bunch of kids to Marrs. He treats Waco like a mother hen. Windy and Solo Sam would give their necks for him. He's a tin god to the Kid. And he ain't trying. It's just natural with him. Could a man like that murder in cold blood?"

She knew a leap of hope. "Then you think he's innocent?"

"I ain't saying that. I guess I'm just waiting, Missus Butler. That's all." He flipped the piece of lead, staring at it. "Just waiting."

The afternoon crawled by, thick with dust, simmering with heat, with the Choctaws always on the horizon. Marrs would not allow anyone to take the chuck wagon far enough ahead so they could set up camp and have the meal ready by the time the herd arrived. He said it was better to stick together and be late with the food. It was dusk when they halted at a sink in a shallow green valley. Dusk, with not enough light left to silhouette those figures on the hills. It seemed even worse than being able to see them.

Marrs said they would have to double the watch on the herd, and put four men out to circle riding. Then he began to prepare the meal. He seemed unhurried as usual, scooping the sourdough swiftly from the keg, pouring water off the beans, dumping them in one skillet. But in the way his eyes pinched together at the edges, in the little muscles drawn tightly at the corners of his lips, Gail could see the strain his double responsibility was building up in him.

167

"Why do you not prepare some decent food for once?" *Don* Vargas muttered. "I would like at least one more good meal before those *Indios* lift my scalp." He leaned back in his saddle, eyes rolling heavenward. "I am thinking of *aves rellenas adobadas y asadas*. I am see it now. A fresh chicken, stuffed with raisins, drenched in toasted red chile sauce . . ."

Marrs banged the pan down on the corrugated iron so hard the *clang* made them all jump. "You're getting pinto beans and java. If you don't like it, you can go out and eat fried dog with them Choctaws!"

There was a moment of strained silence. Then Windy cleared his throat, trying to chuckle. "What are we all so jumpy about? This ain't half as bad as when Pecos Bill got caught by them Comanches up in the Panhandle. The mosquitoes up there are so big you beat 'em out of the chaparral and they go up on the mountain and throw boulders at you. It gets so hot in the summer they bury the dead men in overcoats so they won't freeze when they git to hell."

"Hobble your jaw and pour that coffee," Pata Pala said.

Marrs turned to him. "Maybe you'd like another wreck pan treatment."

The wooden-legged man subsided with a surly growl. Windy's gap-toothed grin spread all over his wrinkled face, and he continued with a triumphant chortle. "Pecos Bill, now, he'd been driving ten thousand head of cattle from Matagorda to Nome. Right smack in the middle of the worst rainstorm you ever saw, he got jumped by Comanches ten feet tall.

168

They chased him right over a thousand-foot cliff. Only thing that saved him was his rawhide suspenders catching on a tree. But the rain had soaked that rawhide and it kept stretching and stretching. Them Comanches went down to the bottom and started shooting at him. He kept sinking and them arrows kept getting closer and he thought he was dead for sartain."

"What happened?" *Don* Vargas's eyes were big and round.

"Sun came out and them suspenders shrank so fast it throwed him into the air like a slingshot. He come down twenty miles away, safe and sound. Ever since, he wears nothing but rawhide galluses."

"My old man only wore one gallus," Kettle said.

"He must've been a Republican. Reminds me of the time Pecos Bill ran for President on the Republican ticket."

"Just keep your hands off your guns and sit tight," Marrs said.

Gail turned toward the cook, frowning at him. Then she saw him looking outside the circle of firelight. The other men were staring that way, too. She blinked her eyes, trying to adjust them to the darkness out there. Slowly the vague figures took shape for her. She heard Paul let out a whistling breath.

"Don't let them come in."

"Slack up," Marrs said. "They wouldn't have come in this far if they meant trouble." He nodded at the Indians. "*Yukpa. Chata hatak.*"

There was a rustling, and then a sonorous voice came from the shadowy group. *"Yukpa. Miliki okla. Nipi okcha ki tushali."*

"What is it?" Butler asked in a tight voice.

"I gave them greetings, they returned it. They want some more food."

"They keep this up, we won't have any more left for ourselves," Kettle Cory groaned.

Slowly the Indians brought their horses in, with the firelight shining on the old copper of their naked chests, their enigmatic faces. They dismounted, murmuring among themselves, holding tight to their rusty Spencers and their war bows.

"Pothooks," Kettle said, "doesn't it seem like more?"

"Plenty more. And probably others out in that timber, watching us."

"What about Sam and the others on the cattle?" Gail asked.

"I don't know how these Indians got through them," Marrs said. "If Sam and the others get jumped, there'll be shots. That's all we can wait for. I still don't think they'd come right in this way if they meant to attack now. It isn't their way. Just sit tight."

So they sat tight around the campfire, the ring of their faces white and tense in the flickering light. They watched the Indians stolidly eat the bread, the meat, the beans, the coffee that had been cooked for them. When the Choctaws were finished, they belched and patted their bellies and mounted their skittish ponies again and faded into the night. As soon as they were out of sight, Butler exploded.

170

"What is this? What kind of game are they playing?" Marrs shook his head. "I don't know."

"How long are they going to keep it up?" Butler's face was pale and drawn, his eyes unnaturally bright. "We can't go on like this all through the Nations."

"We can do whatever they can do," Marrs said. His voice had taken on a flat tone of command. "If they want a fight, we can fight. The main thing is not to let them get us acting like a bunch of old women. Kettle, you go out and see what happened with the night hawks. I'll throw together some more grub."

Kettle came in later to say that the circle riders were all right, and they didn't know how the Indians had got through them without being seen. Marrs said the answer to that was that they were Indians. The meal was eaten in nervous silence. When they were finished, Windy and Kettle and *Don* Vargas went out to spell the others, who came in to eat. Gail and the Caverango Kid cleaned up the dishes for Marrs while he went out to check the herd. Marrs was not back when they finished, and Gail went to the linchpin to prepare for bed. Butler was shaving by the light of a tallow candle, a broken piece of mirror propped before him on the tailgate.

"You shouldn't have jumped on Pothooks that way," she said.

"He's having a hard enough time as it is."

"You seem quick to defend him. First Slaughter, now Marrs."

"Paul, don't be that way. I thought it was all over. I thought you were feeling so much better." She caught his arm. "Paul, I kept looking back at you in the linchpin today, and you seemed so different, so much more like you used to. It's been so long. I kept hoping . . ."

He pulled away. "Hoping what? How could I look different? I was sick and you know it. If you hadn't fed all that paregoric to Waco . . ."

"Paul!" She couldn't keep the shocked sound from her voice. She was staring at him, wide-eyed. Seeing the look in her face, he must have realized what was going through her mind. She saw him begin to summon the childish rage, saw it begin to seep into his cheeks, yellow as jaundice. Suddenly she couldn't face it any more. She wheeled away from him and walked around the linchpin. The men were in their sougans, but she saw the Caverango Kid's round eyes following her and knew he must have overheard them. She turned away from camp and moved behind the chuck wagon. She stood there, holding onto the lowered tailgate, biting her lip, close to tears. She knew it wasn't the quarrel that hurt her so much. She was used to that. It was more the bitter disappointment of seeing Paul revert once more to his spiteful childishness, after knowing such an intense hope today that he was finally well, that she was seeing him change back to the man he had once been. But she knew she should not have expected so much. It had happened so often this way.

There was a rustling sound out in the darkness. She whirled around, a sudden fear blocking the breath in her throat. But it was Marrs, bringing his whey-bellied mare back in. He saw her and swung tiredly out of the

172

saddle, looking down at the strained expression in her face.

"Paul?" he asked quietly.

She lowered her eyes, staring at her hands, as she clasped them tightly in front of her. "Yes," she said in a subdued voice.

He took her by the elbows, gripping them gently with his hairy, rope-scarred hands. The animal magnetism of him seemed to flow through her like a welcome warmth after a deep chill.

"I'm sorry," he said. "I guess I felt the same way you did. For a while today it looked like he might be changing."

She looked up at him, seeing how well he understood the torment in her. His sympathy seemed to ease the tension, the hopelessness. For the first time, she saw how sunken his face looked beneath the blunt cheek bones, how red-rimmed his eyes were. She was filled with a compassion that swept away her own misery.

"You look so tired," she said. She reached up to touch the blue-black stubble on his jaw. "They haven't even given you time to shave."

It was as if the touch set something off within both of them. It was more than his magnetism now. It was an excitation, stirring deeply within her. She saw the same change occurring in him. The tired look left his face, a faint flush crept up the corded neck, into the bearded cheeks. The lackluster of weariness left his eyes. They began to kindle with those little lights. She seemed drawn toward him. He exerted no effort to pull her in, but she realized they were nearer, standing almost together. The tips of her deep breasts touched his chest. A tremor ran through her body. It was something she had not felt in so many years, with a man. It was what she and Paul had known, so long ago, and what they had lost. It swept all conscious thought from her mind, and left only awareness, awareness of his head, bending toward hers, of her own head, tilting back, of her lips softening and growing full and shaping to meet his. For what seemed an endless measure of time they hung on the brink of it, their lips but inches apart.

Then, as if with the same realization, they moved away from each other. He still held her elbows, but he was at arm's length. The heated flush was yet in his face. His breathing had a thick, husky sound. He seemed to speak with difficulty.

"That wouldn't be any good, would it?"

Her voice sounded small, helpless. "No," she said.

"No matter how he's changed, no matter how long ago you lost what you had . . . it wouldn't be any good."

"No," she said again. She lowered her eyes, feeling sick with some loss she could not even name. "It wouldn't, Pothooks."

His voice had grown almost inaudible. "Even if Paul weren't in the picture."

She felt her eyes raise swiftly. "Why do you say that?"

His hands slid off her arms, his great shoulders bowed deeply. He stared emptily at the ground. "Lee Marrs Benton," he said in a dead voice.

She caught his hands, bringing herself unconsciously closer once more. "Don't say that. I know now it

174

wouldn't make any difference. I believe in you, Pothooks. Whatever you said, I'd believe. That wouldn't have anything to do with it, if Paul weren't . . ."

"If Paul weren't what?" Butler said from behind them.

Gail wheeled sharply. She was still holding Marrs, standing right against him, and she knew the look on her face must have been one of surprised guilt. Butler was standing at the corner of the wagon, a Navy Colt in his hand. His face was dead white and the lips were twisted.

"I thought it was Indians," he said. "Isn't that funny? I heard sounds over here and thought it was Indians. And it was just you, saying that if Paul weren't here, you and the cook could have it all to yourselves."

Marrs pulled free of Gail. "Mister Butler, it isn't how it looks. Missus Butler is too decent for anything like that."

Butler's voice was venomous. "I know how decent she is, running off to some man behind the chuck wagon."

"And who sent her running?" Marrs asked. "Every man in camp knows how you treat her. Do you think she'll take that forever?"

"Shut up!"

"I was too easy on you this morning. I thought you'd finally found the guts to face how rotten you are inside. I thought you really needed help."

"Marrs . . ."

"But you've been doing that all your life. You'd turn to whoever happened to be there. And nothing they could say or do really helped. You'll always be the same, Mister Butler. You haven't got the guts to face it alone. A drop in the beef market, a crew that mutinies over the cooking, a bunch of Indians . . . whatever it is, you haven't got the guts to face it alone."

"Damn you!"

Gail tried to stop Butler as he lunged at Marrs. But his impetus knocked her aside. She saw Marrs throw up an arm and try to dodge. It was too late. Butler's gun came down in a vicious whipping motion that knocked Marrs's arm aside and hit him across the face.

He fell back against the wagon, a bloody stripe across his brow. Gail saw that her husband meant to hit him again, and she lunged into Butler, catching his arm, throwing all her weight against it.

"Paul, stop it, stop it!"

He struggled against her, but he could not throw her free. Finally he subsided, his whole body trembling violently, staring at Marrs with a contorted face. Marrs was still sagging against the wagon, dazed with pain, barely able to keep himself from falling.

"Get out," Butler said. His voice sounded strangled. "You're fired. Get out of my camp."

The crew had been drawn by the sounds of the fight, and stood in a loose semicircle around the chuck wagon. It was Windy who spoke.

"If Pothooks goes, we go."

"You do and I'll kill you," Butler said. There was an insane light to his eyes. "I'll kill the first one of you that rides out of camp after him."

176

Marrs had finally straightened up. He held one hand across his bloody wound, eyes shut in pain. He spoke in a thick, slurred voice.

"You can't leave Missus Butler, Windy. You know that."

The crew shifted around undecidedly, glancing covertly at each other, muttering among themselves. Finally Windy said: "Let him stay, Mister Butler. I don't know what this is all about, but you won't git your herd through without Pothooks."

"If he doesn't start going right now, I start shooting," Butler said.

"Paul," Gail said. "Please!"

"Shut up! If you want to be responsible for his death, just keep on talking. Get out, Marrs, damn you, get out!"

Marrs finally opened his eyes. He glanced once at Gail, and then turned to walk toward his whey-bellied mare, hitched on the rope line with the mules. Gail watched helplessly, afraid to move, afraid to speak. There was a crazy light in Butler's eyes, and she knew the slightest thing might snap him now. The Caverango Kid and Windy went over to help the cook saddle up and boosted him aboard the mare. Then he turned the horse. He looked sleepy now with pain, and kept blinking his eyes. His voice had a strange husky sound.

"You're going to need a piece of advice, if you mean to go on. Whatever you do, stay away from timber. Those Indians catch you in the trees and you'll be cooked."

Butler lifted his gun. "One more word, Marrs. That's all. Just one more word."

Marrs took a deep breath, staring down the muzzle of the gun. Then he wheeled the horse and walked it out into the darkness. Gail covered her face with her hands and began to cry.

"Paul," she said. "You fool, you utter fool."

CHAPTER
THIRTEEN

Marrs did not ride far that night. He was in no shape to. Reeling in the saddle, bandanna held to his bleeding face, he free-bitted his horse out into the darkness. When he felt the first slope beneath him and sensed trees about him, he checked the horse and dismounted. He was still nauseated with pain, but vision was becoming clearer to him now.

He was on high ground, maybe a quarter mile from the camp. He could see the ruby wink of the fires below him, could hear the faraway plaint of a sleepy steer. From somewhere a coyote began to yap on the rim. It epitomized what had kept him from going farther. That might really be a coyote. Or it might be a Choctaw.

He hitched his horse and sat down on the ground, trying to clear his head. It was silent about him now, save for the whisper of wind through the Judas trees. He knew his horse would start snorting if Indians approached; he was safe as long as it was quiet.

He knew he wasn't going to leave the herd. He couldn't desert Gail with so little struggle. But he couldn't go back. Butler would be waiting with that gun. And aside from his own personal danger, any trouble like that in the camp would be the worst thing that could happen. If the Indians meant to jump the herd, a fight among the white men would give them an ideal chance.

All Marrs could do was to wait, to hang on the fringes of the herd, hoping he could avoid the Choctaws, hoping he could get back before they struck. Sooner or later Butler would run into trouble with the cattle. Marrs was certain of that. The man just wasn't capable of handling the herd or the crew. Perhaps the man would then see his error and allow Marrs to return. It was the only hope he had.

He unlashed his saddle roll and settled down against a tree with a blanket wrapped around him and his Whitneyville Walker Colt in his lap. The coyotes were yapping again on the rim. He wondered if Gail could hear them, down in the linchpin.

Thought of her sent a poignant wave of desire through him. It came with no shame, no sense of guilt. A man should feel no guilt for his emotions. What he felt for Gail was simply there, within him, as strong and pure and natural as the wind or the rain. It was how he responded to those emotions that governed guilt or innocence. And they had responded in no way that could bring them blame. They must have realized that when they had pulled away from each other by the chuck wagon. To go on would have violated not only the vows Gail had originally made to Butler, but it would have spoiled what lay between Gail and Marrs. For what they knew could not survive dishonesty or shame. It had to be clean and simple and out in the open. Marrs saw this as a simple truth. He knew that no matter how dead the marriage between Butler and Gail was, he could not go to Gail as long as it still existed.

The night passed slowly, with the pain throbbing through his head. He must have dozed, finally, for when he came awake again, it was dawn, and the pungent scent of wood smoke thickened in the air. A ground fog hung over the cattle until they got on the move, and then he saw them begin to emerge from the smoky mist, a snake-like line of tossing horns and ridgepole backs and catty rumps. But no Indians.

Marrs waited till the herd was almost out of sight, watching the ridges for the silhouette of those bobbing feathers, those scimitar war bows. But the ridges remained empty.

Finally he moved, circling far to the west in an effort to come in on the Choctaws' flank if they were waiting in one of the shallow valleys on that side. But he found no camp, no sign. Then he circled the other way around the herd, carefully following the scant cover of timber, dismounting on each ridge so as not to skylight himself, hiding his tracks in what water he found.

Still he could find no sign of them. He was reluctant to accept the logical conclusion. It seemed almost too easy. But by noon they had not shown up. He watched the camp from a hill. His head ached unmercifully and he thought he had never wanted a cup of strong black coffee so badly. Hunger was beginning to gnaw at his belly like a trapped rat. He saw that Gail was doing the cooking, and he was filled with a strong impulse to ride back. But he could see Butler stalking through the camp like a nervous bantam, and knew the man was probably not cooled off yet.

By nightfall he was nauseated by the pain of his head and his empty belly. But he forced himself to scout the surrounding country once more, knowing Butler wouldn't have the wit to send out a man. He covered every ridge from which the Indians would logically watch the herd, ferreted out every possible campsite they might choose, even followed down the yap of the coyotes. But they turned out to be real coyotes.

At last he stopped, worn out, and settled down in the timber overlooking the cattle camp. Maybe it was true, then. Maybe the Choctaws had finally left.

Gail Butler awoke to a ground fog that lay through the camp thick as milk. The fire's glow was a diffused nimbus in the clammy haze; the *clatter* of pots and pans and the low voices of the crew came as from a great distance. Paul Butler was already gone from the blankets beside her.

As she arose and dressed, her thoughts were of Marrs again. It filled her with an intense loneliness to think of him somewhere out there on the back trail, with no one to ride beside him through all this vast land. How ironic, how bitterly ironic, that they should have been drawn together under such hopeless circumstances. There had been so many men who, seeing the mockery of her marriage to Paul, had made their propositions. Slaughter, and the planter in San Antonio, and a dozen others. And none of them ever kindled the slightest interest or reaction in her. And then this strange man with a dark past had come out of nowhere and touched her as she had never been touched before, not even by Paul. And it didn't even matter now that her marriage to Paul was a sham. She knew him well enough to realize he would never give her a divorce.

It was even significant that the thought of divorce should come so naturally. Before, in the height of their emotional scenes, she had known intense desire to escape. But it had merely been reaction, subsiding soon, repressed by her wish to hold their marriage together. Never before had she so calmly and objectively considered divorce. And never before, she realized, had she allowed herself to see Paul for what he really was: the spoiled son of a rich man who had never grown up, who could never meet the realities of life on his own two feet, who would always seek the aid of others (without really wanting it, or being able to use it), or who would retreat into his neurotic spells of sickness and childish tantrums.

Why hadn't she been able to see it at first, why hadn't she seen a warning of what was to come in those first childish spats during their courtship? It had all been so gay and easy for Paul then, with his father's money unlocking all doors, smoothing the way through any real problems before they developed.

She shook her head bitterly, climbed from the wagon, and did her hair up by the cracked mirror on the tailgate. She saw that the Caverango Kid and Windy had the fires going and the coals piled against the coffee pot, and she went over to cook breakfast. Paul was arguing with Pata Pala and Kettle, dim figures in the mist beyond the wagon. His voice was high and shrill with anger.

"You're taking orders from me, and I say that we move on."

"As long as we're in camp, we're fairly safe," Kettle said. "We've got the wagons to fort up by and we can stick close together. Get us strung out on that trail in this fog and them Choctaws could cut us down one by one without the rest of us ever knowing it."

"But they're gone. You said that yourself yesterday. They weren't in sight all day. They didn't come in for food."

"I don't trust 'em," Pata Pala said. "All we gotta do is wait till this fog lifts."

"Which might be now or never," Butler said. "If we stop every time there's a fog, we'll never get to Dodge. We're moving right after breakfast, and that's final."

He wheeled from them and came toward the chuck wagon, face flushed with anger. Gail realized ironically that this was what she had been waiting to see for years — Paul standing on his own two feet again, taking command of a situation, showing the old arrogance and pride she had once so mistakenly admired. But somehow there was no significance now. It had come too late, and was too synthetic. Only his childish anger was driving him now, pitting him stubbornly and unreasonably against all opposition.

He saw her watching him as he strode up, and a flutter of indecision ran through his eyes. He stopped by the tailgate, glancing back over his shoulder at Kettle and the peg-legged man.

"I was right, wasn't I?" he said in a low voice.

"You've got to think of the crew's safety, Paul," she said. "If there's any chance that they might get hurt or killed, wouldn't it be better to wait a few hours?"

"No!" His head lifted in that old arrogance she knew so well. "I was right. We'd be waiting every morning. They knew what chances they were taking when they signed on for the trail. It's a pretty pass when a man's wife doesn't have any confidence in him." He broke off, frowning at her, biting his lip. She saw a change running through his face as he fought to suppress his anger. He grasped her shoulders, looking into her eyes. "Gail," he said. "That's just it. You've got to have confidence in me. Things are going to be different now. I'm feeling better and things are going to be different." His voice lowered; a look of guilt passed through his eyes. "I was pretty snaky to you in the wagon, after Marrs left last night."

"Let's forget it, Paul."

"No. I really didn't mean what I said, Gail. I was all wrought up. Tell me I was wrong. Tell me Marrs was telling the truth."

She met his eyes squarely. "You know he was, Paul. We did nothing to be ashamed of."

He squeezed her shoulders, looking so sincere, so contrite. "I know it's true. He was right. I've been so low to you. You needed someone to turn to. You were just crying on his shoulder, weren't you? Big brother stuff. Like he said, you're too decent. And I'd turned you away. It was all my fault. It was the sickness. Gail, I wasn't myself, you know. But now it'll be different. You can see. It's wonderful to get back in the saddle again. I'll make it up to you, Gail. We'll forget what happened. Roll out that grub and we'll get those cattle off the bed ground."

She watched him walk away, jaunty as a kid with his first red boots. It was an unbelievable change, one that could happen only with a child. She turned listlessly back to her cooking. That was it. A child. And somehow you couldn't feel angry with a child very long, you couldn't feel bitterness or recrimination. It settled back into apathy, with the fog closing in about her, thicker and thicker.

They had improvised a hitch on the linchpin's tongue. Windy attached it to the axle of the chuck wagon while the Caverango Kid harnessed up the mules. Gail knew her food did not approach Marrs's cooking, but the crew did not complain. After the meal Windy and the Kid helped her wash dishes and pack up. Then she climbed into the chuck wagon. The cattle were already moving off the bed ground, and she drove onto the flank of the herd, the linchpin pitching and *thumping* behind. The steers walked apprehensively through the clammy half light. Gail could see only a few feet ahead of her. Her clothes were so dampened that they clung like paste to her back, and the sounds seemed muffled and eerie coming from the depths of the soupy mist.

They had been on the trail half an hour when a rider appeared out of the mist, coming fast and startling Gail.

It was Windy, pulling up beside the wagon. "You better pull farther toward point, Missus Butler."

"What is it?"

"Kettle saw somebody on the right flank. He thought it was one of us and called. The man didn't answer. He faded and Kettle couldn't find him."

Apprehension sent a chill through her. "Windy . . . ?"

"Don't ask me, Missus Butler. But if it is them Choctaws, this would be a prime place to jump us. You stop this wagon and get that shotgun behind the seat. Hang onto it no matter what else you do. I got to go on back to ride with the Kid. Those horses are one of the things them Indians might go after. Your husband said he'd send Waco back to ride with you as soon as he found him. Solo Sam's pretty close on this swing, too. Just holler if you need him."

He peered closely at her, reluctant to leave, then reined his horse away. She checked the mules, wrapped the reins around the whip stock, and crawled back over the seat. The double-barreled shotgun was under the seat, with a box of shells. She put the box in the pocket of her buckskin jacket and laid the gun beside her on the seat. Then she took up the reins once more.

It was the *thumping* linchpin and the *creaking* axles again, the plaintive bawl of a steer lost in the mist and the muted *clatter* of horns, the sound of Solo Sam's off-key chant coming from nowhere:

I'll git me a Porter saddle,
And a line-back bronco to boot,
A quart of Dogtown whiskey,
And quit this old galoot . . .

Gail sat up stiffly, dropping one hand to the shotgun, as another rider appeared in the mist. Sam? No. The man didn't have his slouch. Then she saw that the horse was solid black; the man was Butler.

"Gail? You all right?"

"I'm all right. Sam's near. Hadn't you better stay at the point?"

"*Don* Vargas is up there."

"Alone?"

She saw something furtive run through his face. He shook his head angrily. "What's the difference? They wouldn't strike the point. It's the horses we're worried about. This whole thing is foolishness, anyway. I think Kettle was just jumpy."

"He isn't the jumpy kind, Paul. If you don't want to stay at the point, why not send Sam or somebody else up?"

"It isn't that, you know it isn't that." He broke off, turning to squint out into the fog, listening. Finally he said: "Why should Sam stop singing? He never stops singing."

She listened a moment. "Maybe we've dropped behind a little too far," she said.

"Whip up the mules, then," he said. "Move in closer."

She urged the mules into a trot and guided them closer to the herd. Finally they settled to a walk of their own accord. She saw that Butler was trying to hear Sam again. There was a waxen color to his face.

"Where is he?" His voice sounded strained, hushed. Suddenly he turned to her. "You think I was right, don't you? I didn't make a mistake."

"I told you what I felt at the time, Paul. You have to think of the crew."

"Maybe we should stop."

"All you have to do is tell them," she said. He sent her an oblique look, then stared up toward the head. Indecision sent its flutter of muscle across his narrow cheeks. "Paul," she said. "If you want me to go with you when you tell them, I will."

"I don't want you to. I can do it myself. I'm not afraid to admit my mistakes." He rode along beside her for another space, staring moodily ahead. She could see the indecision building up in him.

"You'd better do it, Paul," she said.

A gusty breath left him. He turned to her. His face was twisted with anger. But deeper than that was the lost, broken expression in his eyes.

"Gail," he said helplessly. "Gail . . ."

"You drive the wagon," she said. "I'll take your horse and go up and tell *Don* Vargas to stop the herd."

He seemed to settle in the saddle, his whole body shrinking. She saw that he was going to do it, and moved over on the seat so he could climb aboard. At the same time, the shot came.

The mules jumped against their hames in surprise. Gail pulled back on the reins, and that only excited the beasts more. There were more shots, a whole volley, somewhere out in the fog. The mules were plunging and rearing in their harness and Gail was half standing in the seat, putting all her weight on the reins to hold them. She saw Butler's black horse pirouetting frantically beneath him, and realized he was putting too tight a rein on it. Then riders burgeoned from the mist ahead, hazy figures on charging ponies, Choctaws.

An arrow *plunked* through the Osnaberg sheeting a foot from Gail's head. Another plunged into the rump of the off wheeler. The mule squealed in pain and reared, and then plunged against the off leader. It put them all into a frenzy and they lunged against their collars and ran.

Gail tried to pull them down, but it was like trying to stop an express train. She fought to turn the mules, knowing if she could get them into a circle, they wouldn't run away with her. She saw another rider off on her flank, and recognized Butler's black horse.

"Paul!" she cried. "I can't stop them! Get ahead of me and pull them into a circle. It's the only way. Paul!"

But he did not seem to hear her. His horse was running headlong up the flank of the herd, and he was twisted in the saddle, staring with a white face toward the Indians behind. She called again, her voice breaking with desperation. But he disappeared into the fog.

The herd was back of her now. But not the Indians. She heard a turkey-gobble war cry behind, and knew some of them must be following her for the mules. She sawed wildly on the reins in another effort to turn the mules. The leather was cutting through her gloves and her hands burned like fire. She didn't know how long she fought with them. It seemed her arms were ready to drop off.

Then there were trees ahead. The mules veered to avoid them, swinging the linchpin around against a hackberry. There was a violent *crash*, and the chuck wagon jerked so wildly she was almost pitched off.

She realized the linchpin must have been torn loose, for the chuck outfit was racing even faster now. The rest of it was like a wild nightmare. She had no measure of time. She was dazed with the exhaustion of fighting the mules. They topped a rise, and plunged wildly down a slope into more timber. Branches clawed at her. The chuck wagon's stern slued into a cottonwood with a deafening *smash*. She felt the bed tilt and the whole world turned upside down.

She cried out with the pain of striking the ground, then lay in a humming daze with the sound of *crashing* wood and screaming mules filling the air. She finally rolled over, stunned, her head swimming. Her whole body hurt, but there was no searing pain of broken bones.

She saw that the chuck wagon lay on its side, wheels and gear smashed to splinters. One of the mules had torn free and was running away; the other three were fighting wildly to tear out of their harness. One of the leaders was down on his back, legs thrashing, squealing like a pig. Gail saw the shotgun lying on the ground between her and the wagon, and crawled to it. She could hear the tattoo of hoofs approaching from the fog, the husky shouts of the Indians. She stumbled to the wagon with the gun and crouched in the cover of the upturned bed, hoping the Indians would go by in the fog.

The lead mule had finally regained his feet. The animals' excitement was fading. Unable to get free of the snarled harness, they nipped at each other, braying in outraged anger. Then even that stopped, and they stood with their gigantic ears twitching.

That turkey-gobble war cry came again, but there was an answering shout, and the tattoo of hoofs ceased.

The silence came so suddenly it almost hurt Gail's ears. She strained to hear. For a long time there was nothing. Then it came like a whispering, out in the brush beneath the trees.

CHAPTER
FOURTEEN

When the shooting first began, Marrs was on the right flank of the herd. He knew what it was immediately, and put his horse in a plunging run down the slope toward the valley below. There was a wild flurry of shots from ahead, a dim shout, a swirl of motion in the fog that he couldn't define. He passed an arrow sunk into the ground. Then the first ranks of the herd burgeoned up out of the mist, a line of tossing horns and backs like ridgepoles.

He realized he was up near the swing, and wheeled his horse down the line of bawling, excited cattle toward the sounds at the drag. But the shooting had already died down. A horseman raced past him somewhere out in the mist. The earth trembled with a sudden running of many animals. But by the time he reached the drag that was gone, too, and it was ominously quiet. He pushed back of the herd, shouting for Caverango.

"Kid, where are you? Where are those horses?"

He got a dim answer off to his left, and wheeled that way, the Walker Colt gripped tightly in one hand. A forlorn figure came limping toward him out of the eerie mist. It was the Caverango Kid, sobbing like a baby.

"You hurt, Kid?"

"No. Just so god damn' mad I'd like to bust a gut. I couldn't help it, Pothooks. Seemed like there was a hunnert of 'em. Shot my horse from under me the first crack. I couldn't help it . . . I just couldn't help it."

"You're saying they got the horses?"

"All of 'em, the whole cavvy. I swear, Pothooks, I couldn't help it."

"All right, Kid, I know. What about the others?"

"What others?"

"You mean Butler didn't put anybody back here to help you? Those horses were the first thing they'd go for."

"I was the only one on the cavvy."

"Damn him!" A sudden fear shot through Marrs. "What about Gail? Where was she?"

"Somebody up at the point must have picked her up. Those mules took out with her. That husband of hers is goin' to need a clean pair of pants. I never saw a man so scairt. He just spurred his horse and run. I saw her holler at him and he didn't even turn around."

Marrs straightened up, the fear growing so strong it almost gagged him. Without waiting for the Kid to finish, he reined his mare around and kicked it into a headlong run up the left flank of the herd. He hadn't gone far when he heard a horse racing back toward him. He pulled up sharp and saw Butler burst from the fog. The man reined his horse in so hard it almost sat down, tossing its head and squealing in pain. Its black hide was marbled with lather. Butler's eyes were as white and wild as the horse's in his pale face, and he let

194

the animal up off its hocks to dance and spin beneath him.

"Marrs!" he shouted. "Got to get Gail! Those mules ran away with her!"

"Which way did she go?"

"They ran away with her! I couldn't do anything!"

Marrs saw the animal panic in the man's face and kicked his mare against the black and grabbed Butler's shirt front. "You could have tried to get them to circling, damn you. What kind of a man are you? Your own wife, you let her go like that, your own wife . . ." He broke off, bunching the shirt so tightly it was choking the man, lifting him half out of the saddle. "Now which way did she go, damn you? Which way?"

Butler pawed ineffectually at Marrs's thick arm, answering in a strangled voice. "To the west. Somewhere along in here. I couldn't find her."

Marrs let him go before he finished and wheeled his mare around and booted it into a dead run. He saw the Caverango Kid running up from the rear after them, and shouted at him.

"Tell Kettle to stop the herd and hold them tight!"

Then he was past, losing the boy in the mist. He turned parallel to the herd again and bent in the saddle to look for wheel tracks heading away from the cattle. Within a few hundred yards he came across them, chewing up the turf, and turned to follow them westward. He heard the pound of hoofs behind him and didn't bother to pull down to see who it was.

He didn't know how far he had gone, maybe a mile, when he came across the linchpin, over on its side against a tree. Apparently it had torn loose from the chuck outfit in a turn, for the wheel marks of the other wagon went on. He followed them through a saddle in the hills and across the sandy flats of a dry river bottom and into more hills. The fog was wet as rain against his face and so thick that it blotted the wheel tracks from sight a few feet ahead of him. He drove his horse at a dead run up the first slope, the fear in him growing all the time. He met timber before topping the ridge. Dodging through the trees, he heard the first booming shot from ahead. It had a muffled, cannon quality. It was no six-gun, he knew. Then he remembered the shotgun the other cook had left in the chuck wagon.

Reaching the crest, he pulled down his blowing, lathered horse. The *boom* came again, and he saw the gun flash like a cherry-red streak in the fog. The wild bray of a mule followed the gunshot. Marrs could guess what had happened now. It was improbable that Gail had been able to stop the chuck wagon. Those circle mules would halt for nothing. As Marrs swung down to hitch his horse, the pound of hoofs came from behind him again. Butler burgeoned out of the fog, the ribs of his black heaving like a bellows.

"What is it?" he asked hoarsely.

"Gail's wrecked the chuck wagon down there. Some of the Indians must have followed it for the mules. They've got her surrounded."

Marrs couldn't keep the look from his face, and Butler swung off his animal, voice shrill. "All right! For God's sake, a man loses his head for a minute . . ."

196

Marrs hitched his reins with a savage pull. "Does he?"

Butler caught his arm, a wild plea in his voice: "Damn you, what do you want? I admit I lost my head . . . all that noise, that confusion, like a thousand of them jumping on us . . . it could happen to any man. I admit it, Marrs. I was in a funk. I didn't know what I was doing. But now I'm all right. You've got to help me make it up to Gail."

Marrs pulled away. He had been deceived before by this glimpse into the man. Now he saw it for what it was.

"You stay here," he said. "Hold the horses."

"No. I'll be all right now. I've got to make it up to her . . . I tell you I've got to go with you."

"I'm not going to sacrifice Gail for you." The savagery of Marrs's tone cut Butler off. "I'm not going to get you down there and have you break and foul us all up."

"I won't break, I swear it."

"You stay here. Follow me a foot and I'll shoot your legs out beneath you!"

Marrs wheeled away from the man, from the shocked expression of his white face. He moved down through the fog with his gun out. A turkey-gobble cry came from far away to his left. The timber thickened, rising like ghostly spires all about him. There was the eerie feeling of moving through a lost world, with the fog sifting about him. He heard the rustle of brush on his right flank and crouched swiftly in the cover of a Judas tree.

A wraith-like figure seemed to float through the mist fifteen feet ahead of him. He felt his hand tighten about his Walker Colt. But the figure disappeared again, moving southward.

Marrs waited until another booming shot came from the mists ahead, and moved toward it swiftly. He dodged a second ghostly figure in the fog, and finally reached the edge of timber. Ahead, in a dry wash, he could barely make out the wrecked chuck wagon and three mules, fiddling in snarled harness.

"Gail!" he shouted. "It's Marrs! I'm coming in!"

He heard a sharp *rattle* of brush off to his right, and started across the sand in a dead run. When he was halfway to the wreck, there was a soft *snapping* sound behind, the *whir* of an arrow. But the shaft struck the ground far to his right, and he reached the cover of the chuck wagon before the Choctaw fired again.

Gail was crouched behind the wrecked bed, the shotgun in her lap. Beside her hunkered Pata Pala, a six-gun in his gnarled hand. At the surprise in Marrs's face, the wooden-legged man grinned.

"I took out after them Indians that got the cavvy," he said. "When I heard shots over here, I figured one of the crew was in trouble, so I turned off. I should've hitched my horse and come in on foot like you. They got my animal before I could reach the wagon."

"If you'd cut those mules loose in the beginning, the Indians might of been satisfied," Marrs said.

"I didn't think about that. We tried to break out of here once and them Choctaws drove us back."

"Let's cut 'em loose now. Head 'em west. The Indians will chase 'em. We'll make a break to the east."

All the time Gail had been watching Marrs, her wide eyes filled with a great relief. Her face was smudged with dirt and dried blood and her blonde hair was a matted tangle, but she seemed oblivious of it.

"You came back," she said wonderingly. "You never really left at all."

He looked into her eyes, seeing what was there, forgetting Pata Pala, the Choctaws, everything but her in that moment. "No," he said, "I never really left." They gazed at each other an instant longer, then he touched her arm. "Ready?"

Her voice was a whisper. "Ready."

Before unhitching the mules, he hunted through the wreckage until he found the sourdough keg and set it up on end. Pata Pala glared at it.

"You ain't goin' to take that!"

"I'd rather leave my pants behind," Marrs said.

The mules started kicking and biting again when he went out among them. He dodged their wildly lashing hoofs, unbuckling traces and girths and breechings, slapping them on the rumps. One by one they bolted for the trees, squealing angrily. There was a shot from timber, gouging out earth a foot from him. He ran back behind the wagon, grabbing at the keg.

"Let's drag it."

They left the cover at a run, Marrs holding the sourdough keg under one arm. They could hear the whoop of Indians from timber on the other side and knew that some of them had been diverted by the mules. But as they reached the trees on the east edge of the wash, there was a vague movement in the fog to their right. Marrs fired toward it, heard a husky shout of pain. A turkey-gobble cry came from dead ahead; an answer came from their left flank. There was a *rattle* of brush, more arrows *hissing* through the trees. One whipped through Gail's buckskin skirts; another drove into the ground at Marrs's feet. Pata Pala's gun crashed time after time.

"They're all around us and I can't see a one!" he shouted.

It was a crazy run, dodging through the trees, firing into the mist at targets they never really saw. Gail stumbled and almost fell, dropping the shotgun. Marrs caught her arm, shouting at her not to stop for the gun. There was ghostly movement ahead. Gail was on her feet again and Marrs let her go to fire at it. For a moment the sound of shots blotted out everything else, and the greasy smell of black powder permeated the clammy fog.

Then, suddenly, the gun sound was gone, and the labored huskiness of their breathing and the *thud* of their feet on the damp ground seemed unnaturally loud in the silence around them.

"I think we're through," Marrs panted. They had reached the ridge and he pulled up, shouting for Butler. The man answered them from the right.

"Hurry up! They're coming up from this side. Hurry up, damn you!"

They wheeled to run that way and the silhouettes of the horses loomed abruptly, monstrously out of the mist. There was surprise in Gail's face as she saw Butler. Then she stumbled again, sobbing with exhaustion, and fell against the man. Marrs halted, breathing gustily. He suddenly realized that Pata Pala was not with them. He wheeled about.

"Where's Pata Pala?"

"I don't know," gasped Gail. "I thought he was right behind us."

Butler saw the look on Marrs's face and shouted wildly: "Don't be a fool! You said you wouldn't sacrifice Gail for me . . . you can't do it for him. We'll all be killed if you go back! Marrs, don't be a fool!"

Marrs sent him a savage look. "Put Gail on a horse and get her out of here. I'm going back after him."

He ran back down off the ridge, into the mist, into the trees. There was the smash of a shot from ahead somewhere. He called Pata Pala. He got a husky answer from down the slope, and ran toward it. The man stumbled out of the fog, laboring up the hill. With every other step he pitched forward on his face. He got back to one knee, firing at something behind him, then lunged to his feet again. He plunged forward a couple of steps, and fell once more. Running toward him, Marrs thought he was hit.

Then, as the man caught at a tree trunk to pull himself up, Marrs saw that his wooden leg was splintered off near the top.

"One of them damn' Choctaws shot it off," the man gasped. "Why'n hell did you come back? You'd broke through them. Now they're coming up from behind and they'll ketch us again."

Marrs reached him, stopping above the man. For the first time he realized that he still had the sourdough keg under one arm. Pata Pala had dragged himself to one knee, and was looking at it, too. "You can't leave that now," he said.

Marrs let it drop to the ground. He grabbed Pata Pala's arm and hoisted him erect. "I can't take both of you. It's just lucky the crew isn't here. Put it to a vote and I know they'd take the sourdough instead of you."

He broke off at the rattle of brush from behind. Someone called shrilly from their left flank. There was an answering cry from their right.

"They've found us again," Pata Pala said. "We'd better drag our navels."

They began staggering up the hill, Pata Pala's left arm thrown over Marrs's shoulder, his right hand free to shoot. There was more sodden rustling of brush. The air was suddenly filled with a *whir* of arrows. The only thing that saved them was the fog. The Indians were not close enough yet to see them; they were shooting blindly at their sound.

Then one of them burgeoned out of the fog, a wraith of a figure dodging toward them from between two trees, a rifle across his hip. Pata Pala jerked around at Marrs's side, firing.

The figure became a Choctaw, staggering forward a few more paces, painted face contorted, trying to lift the rifle and fire, finally falling. Pata Pala was a heavy man, and Marrs was sobbing for breath as they staggered past the wounded Indian and on toward the

202

crest. There were more sounds on their right and Pata Pala fired into the mist before he could see anything.

"I'm out," he panted.

"Take mine. I think I've got a couple left."

Pata Pala holstered his gun and yanked Marrs's weapon from his belt, firing almost as soon as he got it free. It went off twice, and then the hammer made a hollow *clank* against a fired shell.

But they were almost to the ridge, and Marrs saw the horses again, looming grotesquely out of the mist. Gail was holding the reins of both lunging, frightened animals, fighting to keep them from Paul's hands. He was shouting at her, his voice shrill and panicky.

"You fool, we can't wait! We'll both be killed! They're all around us!"

"Hurry up, Pothooks!" she called. "We're here. Hurry up!"

It all happened in that last instant, while they were still half a dozen paces from the horses. A dark figure lunged abruptly from the mat of trees on their flank. He had a bow up, its string drawn to his ear, its arrow notched. And it was pointed at the one who held the horses, because that was what the Choctaws wanted above all. It was pointed at Gail.

Marrs saw Pata Pala jerk the gun up. But he knew it was empty. He hung there, in a moment of utter helplessness, knowing he was too far away to do a thing. Then, in that static instant which seemed to be an eternity and was really only the broken part of a second, he saw Butler's face, filled with that twisted panic. And heard Butler's voice.

"Gail?"

There was a strange, almost questioning sound to its shrill tone. Then the man lunged blindly across in front of her. And when the arrow whipped through the air, it buried itself to its feathers in Butler, instead of the woman.

A good bowman could have fired five arrows in the air in the space of a minute. But that wasn't fast enough to get the second one off before Marrs rushed the Indian. The instant of shock helplessness was gone, and he let Pata Pala go and threw himself at the Choctaw. The brave had the arrow notched and was drawing the string back when Marrs hit him.

The Indian pitched backward and the arrow popped feebly into the air as they both went down. When they hit, Marrs was on top. He caught the man's long black scalp lock and used it to bang his head against the ground, doing it over and over again, till the Choctaw lay limply beneath him.

He got to his feet, gasping for air, and turned to see Gail kneeling beside Butler. She was not touching him. She was staring with a white, drained look to her face. He lay on his back, staring blankly at the sky.

"He's dead," Gail said. There was no life to her voice. It had a hollow, metallic sound. Marrs took one look at the man, then went across and caught her by the arm, pulling her to her feet. She was not crying. She just covered her face with her hands. A tremor ran through her body.

"Gail," Marrs said.

204

She nodded, still covering her face. They helped her aboard one of the horses. Marrs boosted Pata Pala up behind her. There was a shouting in the timber behind them, a *rattle* of brush surprisingly close. Marrs swung aboard Butler's black and booted it into a run down the other side of the slope, behind Gail and the peg-legged man. They ran for a quarter of a mile, then checked their horses to listen. They could hear no sign of pursuit.

"They got the mules," Marrs said. "I guess that was all they really cared about."

He saw that Gail was sitting, white-faced, staring blankly ahead of her. There was still no sign of tears on her face. She spoke in a hollow voice, brittle with emotion that was pent up inside her by the shock.

"Do you think he knew, in that last moment?" she said.

Marrs studied her. For a moment he couldn't answer. He was trying to identify what had been in Butler's face, besides the panic, in that last moment. He couldn't help remembering that Butler's direction would have taken him up and over the ridge. He found himself looking at Pata Pala. The man met his eyes for a moment. Then his gaze dropped, almost guiltily. Marrs drew a deep breath, looking back at Gail.

"I think he knew what he was doing," Marrs said. "He told me on the way out here he wanted to make it up to you. I guess that's what he was doing."

Her chin lifted. There was a shine to her eyes that came from more than tears. "All the other doesn't matter, then, does it?" she said. "I'll just remember that, about Paul."

"Yes," he said gently. "You just remember that."

CHAPTER
FIFTEEN

Bob Slaughter found Jared Thorne and his jayhawkers somewhere on the Chickasaw Reservation. He found them many miles north of the Red River. He found them three days after Pothooks Marrs had whipped him.

There were two or three fires winking through the velvety dusk of the timber, and fifteen or twenty men gathered around them. Here and there, tarnished buttons glinted brazenly on faded blue coats, or the brim of a forage cap cut its oblique, tight line across the side of a man's head.

There was a bobble among the picketed horses beyond the fire, a sudden stirring and whinnying that should have reached the men. But they were too busy laughing and talking and eating, and only when the rider appeared in the circle of firelight did they jump to their feet, scooping old Springfields off the ground or yanking Navy pistols from their belts. Slaughter sat motionlessly on his jaded line-back buckskin. With the firelight glittering against the icy chill of his eyes and turning his pale mane to gold, he looked like some blond giant just emerged from a primeval forest.

Jared Thorne shouldered his heavy way to the front. He had not drawn his gun, but his scarred, calloused hand was on the butt of it, sticking from his belt. Rickett was at his side, and, when he saw who was sitting the horse, a nasty smile fluttered his lips.

"Well, Bob. You get caught in a stampede?" Thorne started to pull his gun, but Rickett laid a restraining hand on his wrist. "Wait, Jared. I think our trail boss has finally come to talk business."

Slaughter felt anger churn through his belly at the reminder of the fight. The remnants of it still had not left him. The scars were not yet healed on his cheek bones and jaw bone, and one eye was still puffy and closed. His ribs ached so much the slightest movement was pain. It was an effort to speak through his cut, bruised lips.

"You still want the Pickle Bar driven to Ellsworth?" There was a chill, ugly light in his eyes.

"Yes." Rickett nodded, smiling wryly. "Yes, I suppose so."

"My way?" said Slaughter.

"What is your way?" said Rickett.

"Leave my cattle and the girl alone," said Slaughter.

"Your cattle?"

"Yes," said Slaughter, something dogged entering his manner. "I've driven them clear from the Nueces, Rickett. I've bottle-fed calves and coddled sick heifers. I've sung to them at night and fed them every day and fought with every trail boss along the Chisholm for the best bed grounds. And then what does she do?" The focus of his eyes had changed, looking beyond the men, and he seemed to be talking to himself more than to Rickett. "She takes up with some damn' cook they pull out of a greasy spoon in Dallas. She wouldn't even believe I hadn't sold out to you. None of them would. Well, now I don't give a damn. I've quit the Pickle Bar and I owe no allegiance to anybody but Bob Slaughter. And no damn' grub-spoiling, pot-hooking coosie is taking over my cattle halfway up the trail. I'm driving them through. Do you hear? I'm driving them through."

"All right, Bob, all right." Rickett laughed placatingly. "Light down and we'll talk about it."

"What about Thibodaux?"

For a moment the sly humor left Rickett's face. Then he shrugged. An oily chuckle escaped him. "You get this herd through to Ellsworth and we'll forget about it. I must admit I never thought anybody could beat Thibodaux to the draw. But if he was too slow, that was his bad luck. Good enough, Bob?"

"Good enough," Slaughter said, stepping off his horse with a great effort. His face had not been washed, and formed a grisly mask of cut, bruised, puffy flesh crusted with dried blood. His shirt hung in tatters from his massive torso, and he walked with a decided limp.

"What did happen to you, Bob?" Rickett asked.

"That's none of your damn' business!"

The crackling savagery of Slaughter's voice made Rickett step back a pace, surprise widening his eyes. Slaughter limped over to a pail of water they had carried from the river and began sloshing his face.

He had no clear memory of the time since he had left the Pickle Bar camp. The first day he had spent in a daze, sick from the beating, sleeping the next night without blankets in the forest. He didn't even remember when he had come out of it and had begun hunting for Rickett and Jared Thorne. He had met a couple of wild horse runners who had seen the jayhawkers traveling west, and had gone into Chickasaw land after them. Hunger gnawed at him now, and no amount of washing would take the smarting pain from his face. But greater than the hunger and pain was his rage. There was but one driving thought in his mind: to get Pothooks Marrs. Even more humiliating to him than the beating was the knowledge that another man should finish his drive north. He would be laughed at from Fort Worth to Dodge City. He would be a standing joke along the trail. *You know Bob Slaughter, the man who got his herd taken away from him by a cook. A damn' cow-camp belly cheater. A son-of-a-bitching sop-and-taters gut robber.*

Viciously Slaughter tore the shreds of his shirt from his back. "You got something for me to wear?"

"Sure, sure," said Rickett. "Get him a shirt, Jared. What's this about leaving the woman alone?"

"Just that," said Slaughter. "Those cattle are still Pickle Bar. All I want is to get rid of that crew." His lips flattened across his teeth. "And leave that cook to me."

"Marrs?" Rickett's grin was malicious. "Gladly." He studied Slaughter's face. "And after we settle that?"

Slaughter nodded, taking the shirt Thorne handed him. It was old denim, for a smaller man, and it split

210

across the laced bulk of his shoulder muscles when he put it on, but that didn't matter. He got something to eat from the fire, and then his eyes roved over the men. They were the scum of the Nations. A few of them were probably deserters from the Army, or murderers running from the law. But the bulk of them were true jayhawkers. They had ridden with Quantrell and his guerrilla raiders during the war, masquerading as Northern soldiers to raid and plunder one town, then switching to the uniform of the South to loot and pillage another. No telling how many men had died before their renegade guns, how many women had been violated, how many homes had been put to the torch. And with the cessation of hostilities and return of law and order to Kansas, they had been pushed west, where they found another lawless country in which they could rob and plunder and kill with impunity. Slaughter was used to hard men, but he still couldn't help feeling a reluctance to work with this gang. He didn't think he had ever seen such an evil-looking lot. Their clothes were tattered and greasy, stained with food and the red clay of the bottoms. They were bearded, for the most part, and their hollow-eyed faces emanated the hungry wolfishness of the wild and the hunted. And yet he knew this was the only way it could be done. "Jared's with you, isn't he? Any of these men ever punched cows?"

The laugh that shook Jared Thorne's chest was rough and humorless. "I guess they've done about everything."

"They can be my crew, then," said Slaughter. "If you want those cattle in Ellsworth, you can give me this bunch to do it with. Marrs was heading for open country. They'll have those cattle herd down the Red to the west. If we can hit them before they leave the blackjacks, it'll be easier."

"Can we, now?" Thorne said. His eyes were small and mean as he reached up to touch a livid scar on his face where Slaughter had kicked him back at the Station House. "I don't know as I'm taking any orders from the likes of this one, Rickett."

"If I can forget what happened back on the Red, you can," Rickett told Thorne.

"But we were planning to hit the Pickle Bar when they reached the Canadian anyway," Thorne said. "Why bring Slaughter in on it?"

"Because we only meant to try and scare them back to the trail to Ellsworth," Rickett said. "This way we get what we want in one blow. It was Slaughter's reputation I wanted in the first place. Once we take over and it gets back to the Red River that Bob Slaughter is driving the Pickle Bar to Ellsworth, a dozen other herds will follow. Don't worry about your end, Jared. We'll give your gang the run of the town when we hit Ellsworth."

Slaughter saw the avid look that came into the gaunt faces. Thorne tugged moodily at his beard, staring at Slaughter from beneath his shaggy red brows.

"All right," he said finally. "But don't try and twist this up on us, Slaughter. We'll tie you to a cactus and let the crows pick out your eyes."

Slaughter's cut lips pulled flat against his teeth, and he looked at the scar on Thorne's face again. "Maybe

212

you're forgetting what happened back at the Station House."

"That's just it," Thorne said. "I ain't forgetting."

"Slack off," Rickett told them. "You both stand to gain by working together. Let's forget the past. Let's ride."

Slaughter turned his ice-blue eyes to the man. "Yes," he said. He was thinking of Pothooks Marrs. "Let's ride."

CHAPTER
SIXTEEN

It was a miserable trip for the Pickle Bar from those foggy hills where Paul Butler had died to Big Bog Crossing. They repaired the linchpin so it could travel, and tried to make a chuck wagon out of it by putting a brace under the tailgate and taking one bunk out of the rear. But all they had for food was the beef on the hoof.

Gail drove the linchpin the rest of that first day. She seemed numbed by Butler's death, strangely withdrawn from Marrs. The Caverango Kid had to ride in the wagon with her, for he was without a mount. Pata Pala was riding Butler's horse on swing, and, with the cavvy gone, the rest of the men had only one animal apiece.

They were jumpy and apprehensive, watching out for the Choctaws. But apparently the Indians were satisfied with the horses, for they did not show up again. That evening they made camp on a flat of bunch grass, with buffalo chips for fuel. Marrs slaughtered a steer and fed them a double order of steaks. But they felt the lack of coffee keenly.

"I would give a hundred *pesos* for one cup of coffee right now," *Don* Vargas said. "I would almost rather have coffee than *aves rellenas*." He frowned. "Well, maybe not really. There is nothing in heaven that compares with *aves rellenas*."

"Ah," groaned Waco, "I heard you cook that chicken so much I'm leakin' leaf lard out of my ears."

"Reminds me of the time Pecos Bill saddled up a chicken and rode it to Galveston," Windy said. "It was the year of the big flood, and Pecos . . ." The old man trailed off, gaping at Pata Pala, as if waiting for something. Finally he asked: "You ain't gave up, have you, pegleg?"

Pata Pala was sitting against a wheel of the linchpin, fashioning himself another leg from a cherry-wood spoke. He looked up at Marrs. He glanced down at his splintered wooden stump. Then he grinned broadly.

"Windy, as far as I'm concerned, you can tell those yarns from here to Christmas, and it'll be music to my ears."

"It better be," Waco said sourly. "From what I hear, you're living on borrowed time as it is. If we don't find a sourdough keg at the next town we hit, we'll take you back and trade you in to those Choctaws for our old keg."

Windy chuckled. "Looks like that's the end of your troubles with this crew, Pothooks. Pata Pala was the last holdout."

"What about *Don* Vargas?" Marrs asked.

"Cook me *aves rellenas*, I follow you to China," *Don* Vargas said.

"Don't be crazy," Windy said. "Where's he goin' to find a fresh chicken out here? Just let me tell you what Pecos Bill did with that chicken in Galveston . . ."

Marrs saw that Gail was not in sight, and left the men, walking behind the wagon. She stood against the back wheel, staring out into the night.

"I wish I could say something to help," he said.

She put a hand on his arm, clutching it tightly, as if in need for some contact. Her voice was husky and strained. "I'm so mixed up, Pothooks. I should be able to cry. I couldn't when he died. I thought it was shock, I thought the crying would come later. But it hasn't come. It's like an emptiness inside me. It's like an ache I should feel and can't."

"Maybe it's because it wasn't really today that you lost Paul," Marrs said. "The man you married really died years ago."

She looked up at him, as if seeking the truth in his words. Some of the confusion seemed to die in her eyes. "Maybe you're right, Pothooks. It's almost as if I didn't know the man who died today."

"Then don't blame yourself for not being able to feel any grief. It's natural for a person to hang onto the past. But there comes a time when we've got to let it go. It took you a long time to face what Paul really was. When you finally admitted it, you realized how long you'd been fooling yourself." She lowered her head, nodding. He pulled her gently around to face him. "Then don't fool yourself about this, Gail. The man who died out there today was just a bad memory from a long time ago. I guess neither of us blame him for what he was. But it's over now. There's no use trying to manufacture grief or loss that isn't there. That would be no more honest than lying. The sooner you get Paul out of your system, the better."

With her head still bowed, she came against him softly. "You seem to understand so much, Pothooks. Talking with you makes me see it so much more clearly."

Her deeply indrawn breath swelled her breasts till they were a silken, cushiony pressure against him. Her nearness stirred the passion in him, filled him with an aching need for all her ripe maturity. But he knew it was not time yet. No matter what a sham her marriage to Butler had been these last years, it would still taint what lay between them now to turn to each other on the very day the man had died. The conventions of the world in which they lived were too strong to be overcome so quickly, even though what Gail and Marrs felt was honest and guiltless. So there would have to be time. And after it had passed, they would know it, and could come to each other.

Then something bitter welled up to shatter the surety within him. What did it matter if the vestiges of her life with Butler still stood in their way, if time would bring them together? How could he even think in those terms? He had been so busy trying to soothe her that he had forgotten the deeper gulf that separated them.

He was still Lee Marrs Benton. No amount of time could change that. Even with Butler gone, he had nothing to offer her. He felt his shoulders sag, felt the lines about his mouth deepen. Her head was still bowed, but she must have felt the subtle change in his body. She looked up. "What is it?"

He tried to veil the bitterness in his face. He clasped her arm with one hand. "Nothing. I've got to go see about the night hawks. Try to get some sleep. Everything will be all right."

She started to say something, but he turned away. He couldn't face her any longer. It seemed such a mockery that he could ease her ache, clear her confusion, when he was so tormented himself.

It was red clay land up near the Washita, rusty as old iron in the morning, bright as lipstick at noon, crimson as blood in the sunset. It was clammy and viscid from spring rains and it sucked at the hoofs of the animals and dripped constantly from the rolling wheels and caked like paste on the boots and clothing of the men. The third morning after Butler's death they met a Mexican boy on the trail. He could speak no English and Marrs got *Don* Vargas to talk with him. When they asked him where he came from, he said his father had a ranch back in the timber.

Marrs took *Don* Vargas and a steer and went with the boy, hoping to barter the beef for other food. They came upon a miserable log shack with chickens scratching in a hoof-beaten dooryard and a pair of Mexicans in filthy cotton shirts and buckskin leggings lounging in the doorway. There were chiles drying on a rack at the side, and an enormously fat woman grinding cornmeal in a *metate* next to it. As Marrs and *Don* Vargas pulled their horses to a halt, *Don* Vargas's eyes widened.

"Look, *pollos*," he said in a hushed voice.

He swung off his horse and ran around the hovel after the chickens. The Mexicans lost all their indolence, jumping to their feet, as a shrill *cackling* sound came. Marrs could hear *Don* Vargas cursing in Spanish, and the pound of his boots across hard ground. One of the Mexicans began running toward the corner of the house. A fat chicken skidded around from the other side and he tripped over it and fell on his face. *Don* Vargas came running after the chicken, jumping over the fallen man, shouting at Marrs.

"Catch him, Marrs! Look at that . . . *aves rellenas* on the hoof! Don't let it go by!"

Marrs wheeled his horse around and blocked the chicken off so that it had to turn in against the house. *Don* Vargas threw himself across the fleeing bird, pinning it to the ground. Panting, laughing triumphantly, he lay across the protesting chicken and bargained with the astonished Mexicans for it. Finally they agreed to trade the chicken, a sack of cornmeal, a dozen strings of chiles, more onions, and a bag of coffee for the steer. They had to speak in loud voices to be heard over the *squawking* of the chicken, and before they had finished there was a *thumping* from within the house. A man came to the door, blinking sleepily.

"What the hell's goin' on, Esteban? I thought you said you'd let me get some shut-eye . . ."

He broke off as his eyes became accustomed to the strong light and he saw Marrs there, sitting the horse. Marrs had not moved or spoken, but he had recognized the man instantly. Narrow enough to take a bath in a shotgun barrel, face sharp as a hatchet, hat and duck

219

jacket and buckskin leggings still spattered with mud and filth — it was Guy Bedar. The blood drained from his hollow cheeks, leaving them shallow as death. He caught at the doorframe with one hand, and his voice sounded brittle.

"What the hell are you doing here?"

"Not tracking you down, if that's what you're afraid of," Marrs said. He glanced around the clearing. "Riding with Rickett now?"

Some of the color returned to Bedar's cheeks, along with his habitual insolence. "I don't even know where he is."

"We'll probably meet a couple more herds around Spavin Creek," Marrs said. "I'm going to pass the word, Bedar. You won't get another job with a trail outfit."

"All right," Bedar said. "We understand each other."

Marrs looked carefully at the two Mexicans. They didn't seem to understand what was going on. "If we're through with the bargaining," he told *Don* Vargas, "lace up that chicken and let's drag it."

They tied the chicken's feet together and slung it behind *Don* Vargas's saddle. Marrs put the meal and the other food behind his saddle, and they rode away. Bedar stood in the doorway, watching them go.

Marrs pushed hard once they were in timber. He told Kettle and Solo Sam about it when they got back to the herd, and sent them out to scout a circle around the outfit. But they found no sign of Rickett or Thorne's jayhawkers.

They made camp that night on the south bank of the Washita, meaning to cross it the next morning. They had tied the chicken at the rear of the linchpin. With the fires ready, Marrs told *Don* Vargas to take the chicken around the wagon and kill it. He had a hatchet and searched for a flat rock on which to position the chicken's neck. The crew stood in a cluster by the fire, waiting. Solo Sam's face was twisted into a scowl.

"That's the cutest little bit of bird I ever seen. Fat as a baby."

"Yeah." Waco rubbed sadly at his sore belly. "I don't know if I'll be able to eat it or not."

But no chopping sound came. In a minute *Don* Vargas walked back into view, holding the chicken under his left arms, the hatchet in his right hand. There was a woeful expression on his face.

"Pothooks," he said, "how can I do it? So plump, so innocent. Look at those eyes. Like my own mother looking up at me." He held the bird out to Windy. "You do it. There ain't nobody as crusty as you."

Windy took the chicken, glanced scornfully around the circle, and disappeared behind the wagon. *Don* Vargas fidgeted around, wringing his hands. The others looked uncomfortable. Then Windy appeared once more, still holding the chicken, shaking his head.

"I can't do it. There's somethin' almost human about it. I wouldn't kill a human being in cold blood."

"We'll never have dinner if you can't kill this damn' chicken," Marrs said. "Give it to me."

He took the chicken, behaving with a docile resignation, and took the hatchet, and went around

221

behind the wagon. He looked down at the chicken. Cussed little jasper. There was something appealing about it, looking up at you, so wide-eyed and innocent.

Hell. He spat. *What's the matter? Going soft or something? I've butchered enough chickens. Man's got to eat if he's going to live.*

He lowered the chicken to the rock, holding it by its feet while he raised the hatchet. But somehow he couldn't bring it down on the chicken's neck. He didn't think he could sleep tonight if he beheaded it. He thought those big solemn eyes would haunt him.

Then there was an agonized shout from the other side of the wagon, and *Don* Vargas ran around and caught his arm. "Please, Pothooks, I can't stand it if you do it. Let it live!"

Marrs made a disgusted sound. "You been complaining about those *aves rellenas* all the way north from San Antonio, and now that you got the chance . . ."

"I'll never ask for *aves rellenas* again." *Don* Vargas dropped to his knees by the bird, putting his arms around its neck. "Why should I? *Buey.* If we eat it, I only have *aves rellenas* one night. Let it live and I have it every day of the year. That's what it is. A walking *ave rellena.* Just one look at it is as good as a whole meal."

"I never saw such a bunch of old mother hens," Marrs said.

Gail caught his arm as he walked back around the wagon. "I'm glad you didn't do it," she said.

"I guess I'm soft, too," Marrs growled. "I couldn't chop off its head."

222

So they had steaks and pan bread again. But they had onions and chile sauce for the meat, and coffee to wash it down. It put the crew in better spirits than they'd been in since they had lost the chuck wagon, and after dinner they sat around fondling and teasing the chicken like a bunch of kids with a new puppy. But Marrs couldn't get Bedar out of his mind. After a while he took Solo Sam aside.

"How about a special watch tonight?" he said.

The man grinned. "Anything you say, Pothooks."

"I'll ride it till midnight. You relieve me then," Marrs said. "There's open country on our left flank. If anybody jumps us, it won't likely be from there. The timber on our right's the logical spot. I want you to take that sixteen-shot Henry of yours and cruise the trees about a quarter mile west of us. If anybody comes through, don't fight 'em. Just get back here as quick as possible and let us know."

"You mean Jared Thorne and his jayhawkers?"

"Or Bob Slaughter," Marrs said.

CHAPTER
SEVENTEEN

There were twenty men. They had been riding three days when they reached the cabin of Esteban Miranda in the clearing fifteen miles south of the Washita. It was after midnight, with a moon winking from behind scudding clouds to cast inky shadows beneath the Judas trees and warped hackberries. The horsemen *clattered* into the dooryard with a great snorting of animals and creaking of gear. Jared Thorne was first to pull his lathered mare to a halt, speaking roughly to Harry Rickett.

"Esteban and me've been doing business for years. He'll know if Pickle Bar passed here and he'll know what shape they're in."

Bob Slaughter took out a filthy bandanna and scrubbed wearily at the grime caked on his face. "That's what we want. If Marrs has made a big enough botch of things, we can just walk in without a shot fired and take over."

"Maybe he'll surprise you," Rickett said.

"The hell with that. Handling a trail herd's in a different world from slinging hash."

The door was open, and Thorne said: "Esteban?"

"*Sí.*"

"*Es Jared. ¿Qué tal? Digame lo qué quiero saber. ¿Los hombres del Pickle Bar . . . ?*"

"*Sí, sí,*" the Mexican grumbled. "*Pasan hoy. Y aqui es un amigo de su.*"

"What is it?" Rickett asked.

"I asked him to tell me about Pickle Bar," Thorne told him. "He said they passed by today. Says a friend of mine's here."

He broke off as the other man stepped into the doorway. Moonlight sank black hollows beneath his sharp cheek bones, made his eyes look like the sockets of a skull. Rickett leaned forward in his saddle, staring at him.

"Where the hell have you been, Bedar?"

"Hunting you," Bedar said querulously. "Figured I was through on Pickle Bar when Marrs took over. He knew my connections with you. I couldn't find you along the Red. I knew you'd probably be passing here sooner or later."

"If Pickle Bar passed by today, they can't be over ten miles ahead," Slaughter said. "Let's hit them."

"A little caution," Rickett said.

"Why?" Slaughter asked. "The whole crew hates Marrs. Minute they learn I'm here, they'll be with us."

"Not quite the whole crew," Bedar said. "That cook is the Caverango Kid's little tin god."

"And remember what Marrs did for Solo Sam," Rickett observed.

"All right." Anger gave Slaughter's voice a raw edge. "So maybe the Kid and Solo Sam. A kid and a gutless string bean that doesn't know enough to come in out of the rain. What does that give Marrs? Pata Pala hates his guts. Waco won't have nothing to do with him."

"Cool off, Slaughter," Rickett said. "Do you always have to ram head-on into things? I want this to be the finish, and I want it to be right. They probably made Big Bog Crossing. The herds usually camp on this side and cross in the morning. There's open country to the east, timber on their west flank. If we move in through that timber, we can probably get close enough to see the layout and jump right down their throats before they know what hit 'em."

"Whatever we do," Slaughter said, "let's get on it."

He sat heavily in the saddle for a moment, watching Bedar go for his horse, feeling weariness like a great weight pressing against him. Then he shook his head savagely and wheeled his horse and galloped out through the trees. The hell with Bedar. Let him catch up if he could.

Slaughter heard the other riders lining out after him. The wind refreshed him and the pound of his blood began to answer the pound of hoofs and the knowledge that he would soon meet Marrs resurrected the raw anger that had been smoldering in him all the way north, till there was nothing left in his mind but the driving need for vindication and revenge.

They rode the best part of the night out and came in sight of the timber near dawn, a dim silhouette stretched across the horizon. They circled to the west of the crossing and entered the trees near the river. It was patchy timber, dense stands of cottonwoods and hackberries interspersed with open parks.

They slowed down and spread out a little. Slaughter could see more tension in their slouched figures, their hungry faces. They filtered through one stand of trees and across an open park. Dawn light began seeping through the foliage, milky, eerie.

"How much farther?" Rickett asked in a hushed tone.

"Don't ask me," Slaughter said. "I've never been this far west."

They moved into another park, where the buffalo grass was jeweled with dew. Slaughter was halfway across when a sudden movement came from timber on the other side. Slaughter caught the dim patches of a paint. There was only one man on Pickle Bar who rode a paint night horse. Realizing the man had already seen them, Slaughter didn't bother to keep his voice down.

"It's Sam!" he shouted. "They must have put him out on watch. Don't let him get back."

He spurred his buckskin and heard men shouting around him. There was the detonation of a shot. One of the men on Slaughter's flank pitched out of the saddle with a broken cry. Slaughter had his six-shooter out now, and he threw down on Sam. His second shot hit the paint, and he saw it tumble in the trees.

But Solo Sam kicked free and jumped before it went down, light shimmering down the barrel of the rifle he held in one hand. He hit rolling and flopped up to one knee and began firing. A horse screamed shrilly behind Slaughter and the earth shook as it fell.

Slaughter fired again at Sam, but he had reached the trees. He reined aside to avoid a hackberry and the rump of his veering horse slapped into a cottonwood, almost pitching him. He had to pull his horse in so hard he screamed in pain and spun around. The timber was packed too densely to run through, and the other riders were having trouble. Sam was adding to the frenzied confusion with his rifle.

Just as a pair of Thorne's men reached timber, trying to pull their horses down to avoid smashing into the trees, one of Sam's bullets hit the right horse. It veered into the other animal and they both went down in a squealing, kicking tangle. A third man behind tried to veer aside and ran headlong into a Judas tree, going over the head of his horse. A fourth man took one of Sam's bullets in the chest and threw up his arms and fell back over the rump of his horse, and the riderless animal ran frantically through the trees toward the river.

The dense timber and Sam's devastating fire had broken the jayhawkers' concerted drive. Half of them were held up at the edge of the trees, milling around in confusion, and the ones who had gained the timber were breaking before the deadly hail of Sam's Henry.

"Scatter, damn you, and get around him through the trees!" Slaughter bellowed.

But they didn't answer his order. Cursing, he tried to fight his excited buckskin around and drive it after Sam, firing at the man again. But Sam made a poor target, farther away now, backing through the shadowy timber in the dawn light. A limb swept into Slaughter's vision and he bent double over his saddle to keep from being knocked off.

As he came erect again, he saw that he had lost sight of Sam momentarily. He reined his horse in, spinning it, trying to find the man in the treacherous light again. A jayhawker came galloping in from the flank, shouting excitedly.

"There's more coming in from the east, Slaughter! They're all around us!"

He broke off as a gun roared from the trees. He jerked in the saddle and slid sideways off his horse and struck a tree and hit the ground and flopped over on his back. There was a wet red patch in the middle of his chest and his mouth was gaping open foolishly. Slaughter was already wheeling his horse to find who had killed the man. There was a second shot, and his hat was whipped from his head. Then Slaughter saw Pata Pala coming toward him on foot, throwing down for another shot. Slaughter fired in sheer reflex action. Pata Pala shouted in pain and fell heavily on his face. At the same time Slaughter heard Waco Garrett's vinegar voice from directly behind him.

"Now I'll send you to hell on the same shutter!"

CHAPTER
EIGHTEEN

Gail had still been asleep in the linchpin when the firing began in the timber. She had awakened to the din and had hurriedly pulled on a buckskin skirt and a blouse, taking the shotgun with her as she climbed out. The camp was full of men running every which way. The Caverango Kid came charging through the tumbled, empty sougans, panting at her.

"Marrs and them are already in timber. He told Kettle to side Windy on the herd. I'm supposed to stay in camp with you. If they get through Marrs, we hold them off till Windy and Kettle can run the herd in the river. Marrs says a mill in the water's better'n a stampede."

"Who is it?"

"I don't know. Marrs thinks jayhawkers."

He broke off at the rattle of renewed firing out in the timber. Dawn light made a misty half world of the camp. Kettle Cory's horse was spooked by the gunshots and he was having trouble getting his saddle on the jumping animal. He had just thrown the kak aboard and was pulling the cinch tight when a pair of riders burst from the trees near the river. They pulled to a rearing halt, as if in surprise.

"They're getting through!" the Caverango Kid shouted wildly. "We'd better put that herd in the river. They're getting through!"

Gail caught his arm and pulled him behind the linchpin as the men began firing. Holding the reins of his lunging horse in one hand, Kettle pulled his gun with the other and returned their fire. He knocked one man out of the saddle with his second shot. The other tried to swing his animal around and it stumbled and threw him.

He hit hard, rolling over, coming to his knees, crawling for the trees. Kettle fired again, but missed. The man gained the trees and turned around there, still on his hands and knees, and began shooting.

The trunk of a hackberry blocked him off from Gail. She ran for the other end of the wagon, hoping she could get a shot at him from there. Kettle Cory was reluctant to let his horse go and seek cover. He tried to pull it behind the linchpin, snarling at it.

"You damn' little biscuit cutter, get in behind here before I flay your hide right off your . . ."

The man behind the tree fired again and Kettle's nasal voice broke off with a cry of pain. He released his horse, clutching at his side, and staggered toward the linchpin. As Kettle dropped behind the cover of a front wheel, Gail gained that end. She had a glimpse of the man's shoulder behind the tree and let go both barrels. When the smoke cleared, he was not in sight.

Kettle chuckled weakly. "I don't think you hit him, but you sure as hell scared him all the way back to San Antonio!"

She leaned the shotgun against the wheel, dropping to one knee beside the fat man. He grinned feebly at her.

"I'm all right. They don't make the gun that can penetrate all this leaf lard I pack. He just chipped a little tallow off my short ribs. I won't be able to ride, though. Kid, you better ketch up my horse and go help Windy with that herd."

Kettle's horse had run halfway out to the cattle, and then stopped, fiddling around nervously, its trailing reins ground-hitching the animal. The Caverango Kid glanced at the trees, then trotted out toward the horse. Kettle was squinting out at the man he had shot off the horse.

"Ever seen Harry Rickett before?" he asked.

She stared out at the body of the man, in its crumpled maroon fustian, its flowered cravat. "I've never seen him, but it's the man Slaughter sold out to, isn't it?"

"That's right," Kettle said. "I got something I want to see. You stay here and cover me. I think you cleaned out the timber good enough with that Greener of yours, but there's no use taking chances."

She started to protest, but he had already got to his feet, wheezing with the effort, and was limping out toward the body. It seemed to take an eternity for him to reach it. There was another flurry of shots in the timber. They seemed farther away. Someone shouted huskily from the depths of the grove. She reloaded the shotgun from the box of shells in her jacket pocket. Kettle stooped over Rickett, pulling something from within his coat, and waddled back to the wagon with it. She saw that it was a nickel-plated Derringer. Still gripping his side with one hand, Kettle eased himself down against the wheel. He studied the gun closely.

"It's a Slotter, Gail. Caliber Forty-Seven. You don't find that caliber very often. He had it under his arm, in a sling. When Gary Carson was killed, down by that shack in San Antonio, Harry Rickett was one of the detectives with us. We were all scattered through the timber, none near enough to see the other. We naturally assumed that Benton had shot Carson from the shack. But when I saw Carson's body, I didn't think such a long shot could make such a big hole in a man. I went back and looked around." Kettle fished the chunk of mashed lead from his pocket. "I found this slug just about where it would have dropped after going through Carson if a man had shot him from the trees, instead of the cabin, with a short-barreled gun. More than one gunsmith verified the kind of gun it would come from. A Slotter Derringer, Gail. Caliber Forty-Seven."

She could hardly speak. "You mean Rickett killed Carson?"

"This proves it," he said. "I've been waiting a long time to find out who carried the gun that fits this slug. You see, Rickett was representing the Fort Worth Cattle Company at the time of the killing. But I found out later that previously he had been on Boa Snyder's payroll. Undoubtedly he was still Snyder's man when he killed Carson."

She frowned. "And Snyder was the man who had Lee Benton's death sentence commuted for fear the

233

information against him would be revealed on Benton's death."

"That's right," Kettle said. "And here's the connection. What did Benton's information prove? That Snyder, Curt Young, and a dozen other men who are big now really didn't quit mavericking after it was outlawed. Something like that could ruin them, as well as put them in jail. Apparently they were afraid of the same thing being uncovered by the Nueces County investigation, which had been started when the first Association detective was found tied to a cactus, tortured to death. They had to divert attention from the investigation quick. Gary Carson's murder did it. Maybe Snyder had told Rickett to do it, maybe Rickett did it on the spur of the moment. Either way, he must have known how the public fury would be turned on Lee M. Benton, and how the investigation would die out during the trial."

She turned slowly to look toward the trees, her face pale, her lips bloodless. "Can you pray, Kettle?"

"I never tried."

"Try now. Pray that we haven't found this too late."

CHAPTER
NINETEEN

It was all a hellish racket around Marrs. He was deep in the trees now, with no over-all sense of the battle. He knew that Sam's devastating fire had broken the jayhawkers' first rush, that the Pickle Bar men had come up in time to break the second charge. The timber was Pickle Bar's ally. In the open the jayhawkers would have swept over them. But the trees stood so densely that Thorne's men could gain no momentum.

He could see a dim swirl of horsebackers in the thickets far ahead. He ran past the crumpled body of a man in a gray forage cap and a coat with a sergeant's stripes still on it. He caught a sudden glimpse of *Don* Vargas on his right flank and ahead of him.

"*Don* Vargas!" he shouted. "Don't get too far in front. They'll cut you off."

"Where's my chicken?" *Don* Vargas called.

"The hell with your chicken! Stay with us. We want to drive them out in the open."

"It's out here somewhere. I saw it follow me out."

A *crash* of gunfire to their left broke in on the Mexican. Solo Sam appeared in the distance, face grimed with black powder, frantically levering his Henry.

"Marrs, they're trying to break through over here. My gun's empty."

Marrs wheeled and ran toward the man, aware that *Don* Vargas was following. He saw two horsemen crashing through the trees beyond Sam, one in a military greatcoat, the other huge and red-bearded. Three jayhawkers, on foot, were following them. Still running, Marrs fired. He got the man in the greatcoat with his second shot. The man cried out in pain and tumbled off the rump of his horse.

At the same time, *Don* Vargas came up behind, emptying his gun at the jayhawkers. One of his bullets struck the other horse. It stumbled and pitched the huge red-bearded man. He hit hard, flopped over, stumbled dazedly to his feet, and plunged for the underbrush. Marrs shot at him but missed.

"That's Jared Thorne," *Don* Vargas yelled, and veered to crash into the underbrush after the man.

Marrs was still running forward. He emptied his gun at the three men on foot. He hit none of them, but the fire made them break and seek cover. Then a gun began to go off from behind Marrs. It was Solo Sam, coming up with his Henry.

"It's all right now!" he shouted. "I've got my smoke pole full again!"

At the same time, Marrs saw Thorne break from the brush into a patch of open ground, running for the big clearing to the west. He was stumbling heavily and holding his shoulder, as if he had hurt it in the fall. As Thorne reached the trees on the other side of the open patch, *Don* Vargas ran from the underbrush behind him. The Mexican let out a triumphant yell and threw down on Thorne. But no shot came. Marrs realized the Mexican's gun was empty.

Thorne checked himself, turning. There was a twisted look of vindication on his face as he lifted his six-gun. Marrs felt his own gun jerk up in reaction. Too late, he realized it also was empty. A wave of utter helplessness swept him.

Then there was a *rattle* of brush from Thorne's right, a shrill *cackling*. The crazy sound made Thorne turn involuntarily, and his shot went wild, missing *Don* Vargas. The chicken came crashing out of the brush and ran between them.

Before Thorne could recover, *Don* Vargas threw his empty six-shooter at the man. Thorne tried to dodge and fire, but the gun caught him in the face, knocking him backward and off his feet. *Don* Vargas ran for the man, launching himself in a dive, to land on top of Thorne as he fell. The Mexican wrenched the man's six-gun from his hand. They hit the ground hard, with *Don* Vargas on top. He lunged up over Thorne, hitting the man across the face with his own gun. He struck once, twice. Thorne jerked stiffly, then went utterly limp.

Don Vargas got to his feet above the man, panting. He saw Marrs and grinned. "Who says the hell with my chicken?" he shouted.

"I'll never eat chicken again!" Marrs called. "Now duck your fool head. Those others are still here."

Don Vargas dodged behind a tree and worked his way over to Marrs and Solo Sam, who were covered by the thickets. Then they began to move forward again. But apparently the loss of their leader had taken the heart from the other three, for the Pickle Bar men did not encounter them. Near the edge of the clearing they found Waco Garrett. He was sitting against a tree, holding his belly, and the ground about him was soaked with blood.

He must have heard them coming toward him. His eyes fluttered open. There was not much life left in them. He tried to grin, as Marrs dropped to a knee beside him.

"Slaughter let the daylight through. I had the drop on him, too. He put the spurs to his horse in the last minute and made it jump and I missed my shot. Then he put it to me." Waco leaned his head back against the tree, his voice growing feebler. "You got the ringiest bull in the pasture there, Pothooks. I never saw such sure death with a gun. I don't think anybody else could've done it, from a jumping horse like that." Blood bubbled out of his mouth, and he began to cough weakly. "Too bad I couldn't have some more of that tallow and molasses. It was better'n all the paregoric I ever took."

That was all. His eyes closed. His hands relaxed across his belly, and he slid down the tree till he was flat on the ground. Marrs gazed at him a moment with squinted eyes. Then he got to his feet. There was a terrible look on his face.

"Let's find Slaughter," he said.

CHAPTER
TWENTY

It was farther down toward the river. It was in a cove of bottom lands, in the dubious shelter of a high cutbank. There were six jayhawkers, and Bob Slaughter. Some of them had lost their horses, some had left them. Slaughter had lost his. It had pitched him back there by the clearing, after he had shot Waco. It was only a cow horse, not inured to the gunfire of real battle. The shocking sound and the pain of Slaughter's spurs had put it in a frenzy. He had been too intent upon hitting Waco, and its first wild lunge had caught him off balance.

After that, a flurry of gunfire had turned him on foot toward the river. He had hoped it was more Pickle Bar, but it was only this handful of jayhawkers crouching in the lee of the bank, sniping at vague movements deep in the timber. They had no heart to move back against the cowhands, but they were reluctant to escape across the clearing for fear they would be too exposed in the open.

"Damn you," Slaughter said. "Pickle Bar has lost Waco and Pata Pala. I know, because I got 'em. They had to leave somebody on the herd. That only leaves three or four that could still be in the timber. What better odds could you ask?"

One of the jayhawkers was young, haggard, with a feverish look to his hollow eyes. "Thorne's dead," he said. "I saw that Mexican git him. That string bean's like an army with that Henry of his. I ain't going back in there with this damn' breechloader."

"Yes, you are," Slaughter said. He brought his gun up, pointing it at the man's belly. "If you don't jump to it, I'll shoot your guts out. Now move!"

They stirred sullenly. One of them made a furtive move with his gun. Slaughter swung his weapon toward the man. The jayhawker froze. Suddenly, in a fit of rage, Slaughter wheeled back to the one with the feverish eyes and whipped his gun across the man's face. The jayhawker shouted in pain, staggering backward, and fell in a sitting position against the bank. He clapped both hands to the bloody weal across his face and bent over, sobbing with pain.

"Now," Slaughter told them, "are you going to move, or aren't you?"

Slowly, reluctantly, fear in their faces, they began to climb up the bank. He had to jerk his gun at a couple of them to make them go on. Finally they were in the timber above. He followed them, seeing how nervously they jumped at the slightest sound, how their heads turned constantly from side to side. *What a hell of a bunch to be stuck with*, he thought.

But it was all he had left. If they didn't break through now, they would never make it. There was a shadowy movement in the timber ahead.

"There they are!"

The man beside Slaughter squeezed his trigger and the rest of the guns caught it up like a roar of giant surf. Slaughter saw more movement ahead and snapped a shot at it. The greasy smell of black powder lay thickly on the air and someone was coughing in it. The excitement of battle caught at Slaughter, with the thunderous *crash* of guns and the shouting of men all around him. He found himself running with the rest, shouting with the rest, firing at anything that moved. He saw a lean shape jumping between two trees ahead, and fired, and knew he had missed. Then the man on his flank shouted and fell and rolled over and over and finally came to a stop against a tree.

"It's that string bean with the Henry!" a man shouted, and veered off and started to wheel back.

"God damn you, come back here!" Slaughter yelled. But the man was running, and Slaughter wheeled and shot his leg from under him. "I swear it, I'll kill you myself before I'll let you run. Come back, you yellow bastards!"

But another one was breaking and running, and another. One of them dodged into the trees, turning to fire at Slaughter. The bullet *whined* past Slaughter's head, and he came to a full stop to shoot back at the man. But he missed. Then his towering rage gripped him, and he began running forward once more.

"All right, you yellow bastards, I'll do it alone! I don't need scum like you!" He was sobbing with rage and with the need of air, and the pound of his boots seemed to jar through his whole body. He saw Solo

Sam ahead of him again, and fired, and lost sight of him. There was smoke all around him, black, choking. "Marrs, where are you? I'll kill you! Where are you?"

"Here I am, Slaughter."

Slaughter half turned, still running, to see the man coming at him from behind a pair of hackberries. He shot from the hip and the bucking of his gun jerked it as high as his face. He saw the bullet eat white wood out of a hackberry a foot from Marrs. Then he saw Marrs's gun flame. A tearing pain made his whole body jerk.

He realized his gun was up in front of his face again, and he tried to run on. A second pain burned through him. He threw down his gun again, firing. But he couldn't see Marrs. All he could see was the ground, his bullet going into the ground, and then the ground itself was coming up to him, and then he couldn't see anything any more.

The silence was almost worse than the firing had been. For what seemed the longest wait in her life, Gail Butler stood there beside the wagon, with Kettle sitting against the wheel at her feet, listening, waiting. But no more shots came.

Then Gail heard the faintest *rattle* of someone coming through the underbrush in the timber. Her breath blocked up in her throat. The man came from the trees into the bright morning light and stopped, staring blankly at Rickett. Gail had already let the gun slide from her hands and was running toward him. His broad shoulders were bowed; he looked sodden, utterly drained. She reached him, going into his arms, feeling

242

the tears dampen his shirt, for her face was pressed to his chest.

"You aren't hurt." She kept saying it over and over. "You aren't hurt."

"I'm all right." Marrs spoke with husky effort. "I've got to tell you this. Slaughter killed Waco."

She pressed herself more tightly against him, with the tears coming again. She was surprised that she felt more grief for Waco than she had for Paul. She heard Kettle wheezing as he limped up behind them. Finally, in a low voice, she asked: "And the others?"

"Pata Pala got it in the leg. They're bringing him in. I had to see if you were all right." Marrs paused, and then answered their unspoken question. "Slaughter's dead, too."

For a long space only Kettle's wheezing breath disturbed the silence. Finally the fat man said: "Then it's over."

Marrs looked at Rickett's body. "Is it?"

Gail lifted her tear-streaked face to him. "He means it, Pothooks. Kettle knows who you are. He has the bullet that killed Carson, and it matches Rickett's Derringer. It proves your innocence. You're free, Pothooks."

He slowly pushed back from Gail, staring at Kettle, a million things shuttling through his face. She saw the bitterness and the pain and the defeat of twelve years slide from him. The sullen withdrawal left his eyes, and they looked infinitely younger. He shook his head wonderingly from side to side.

"You old tub of lard," he murmured. "Is that what you were playing cat-and-mouse with me for?"

Kettle nodded, chuckling grimly. "Don't you worry about Boa Snyder and them others, either. I figure you never tried to turn in the information you had on them because you thought nobody'd believe a convicted man. But we couple my testimony and this evidence with what you got, and it'll break Snyder and everyone else connected with it."

Marrs drew in a deep breath. It lifted his shoulders, took the drained look from him. He grasped Gail's arms, looking squarely into her eyes. She knew that but for Waco, he would be smiling.

"You said once that nothing would stand between us."

"Wasn't I right?" she asked softly.

In answer, he pulled her to him again. She remained that way, in his arms, oblivious of Kettle. It was as if all the doubts and confusions and bitterness of a lifetime were driven away, and she felt a greater peace than she had ever known before. Her arms tightened about him, because she wanted to keep it that way, the rest of her life.

About the Author

Les Savage, Jr. was born in Alhambra, California and grew up in Los Angeles. His first published story was "Bullets and Bullwhips," accepted by the prestigious magazine, Street & Smith's *Western Story*. Almost ninety more magazine stories followed, all set on the American frontier, many of them published in Fiction House magazines such as *Frontier Stories* and *Lariat Story Magazine* where Savage became a superstar with his name on many covers. His first novel, *Treasure of the Brasada*, appeared from Simon & Schuster in 1947. Due to his preference for historical accuracy, Savage often ran into problems with book editors in the 1950s who were concerned about marriages between his protagonists and women of different races — a commonplace on the real frontier but not in much Western fiction in that decade. Savage died young, at thirty-five, from complications arising out of hereditary diabetes and elevated cholesterol. However, as a result of the censorship imposed on many of his works, only now are they being fully restored by returning to the author's original manuscripts. Among Savage's finest Western stories are *Fire Dance at Spider Rock* (Five

Star Westerns, 1995), *Medicine Wheel* (Five Star Westerns, 1996), *Coffin Gap* (Five Star Westerns, 1997), *Phantoms in the Night* (Five Star Westerns, 1998), *The Bloody Quarter* (Five Star Westerns, 1999), *In the Land of Little Sticks* (Five Star Westerns, 2000), *The Cavan Breed* (Five Star Westerns, 2001), and *Danger Rides the River* (Five Star Westerns, 2002). Much as Stephen Crane before him, while he wrote, the shadow of his imminent death grew longer and longer across his young life, and he knew that, if he was going to do it at all, he would have to do it quickly. He did it well, and, now that his novels and stories are being restored to what he had intended them to be, his achievement irradiated by his powerful and profoundly sensitive imagination will be with us always, as he had wanted it to be, as he had so rushed against time and mortality that it might be.